the

CAMERA

never lies

the

CAMERA

never lies

Elizabeth Goddard

BARBOUR
PUBLISHING

© 2010 by Elizabeth Goddard

ISBN 978-1-60260-627-2

For more information about Elizabeth Goddard, please access the author's Web site at the following Internet address: www.bethgoddard.com.

Cover design: Faceout Studio, www.faceoutstudio.com.

Published by Barbour Publishing, Inc., P.O. Box 719, Uhrichsville, OH 44683, www.barbourbooks.com

Our mission is to publish and distribute inspirational products offering exceptional value and biblical encouragement to the masses.

 Member of the
Evangelical Christian
Publishers Association

Printed in the United States of America.

DEDICATION

For Dan, Rachel, Christopher, Jonathan, and Andrew.

ACKNOWLEDGMENTS

A special thank-you to Anthony Brisbane Smith, British photographer extraordinaire, for his invaluable input regarding photography and all things British. Thanks to the park rangers at Crater Lake National Park for answering innumerable questions. To Candice Speare Prentice, I'm so grateful for your assistance in police procedures and for putting in a good word for me. And to Susan Downs, thank you for believing in me. To critique partners Lynette Sowell, Lisa Harris, Deborah Vogts, and Shannon McNear—I couldn't have done this without you! To all the writers in the Spyglass Lane Mysteries group, your encouragement and camaraderie keeps me going. Ellen Tarver, you're great to work with, and I appreciate the way you accommodated my sense of humor in this story.

CHAPTER ONE

Everyone I knew except my mother maintained a personal space bubble.

"Polly. . ." Tears welled in Mom's eyes as we lounged outside at the Terrace Café, which overlooked Caldera Lake. "I've lost a great deal of money." Her features drooped.

Mom's bubble was more like a space dome, where everyone was invited in and welcomed to her conversation. I studied her. Looking uncomfortable under my scrutiny, she sighed and shifted in her seat before slumping against the wicker chair back. Though she was no stranger to melodrama, she'd never seemed this distressed. Not even the innumerable other times someone had taken advantage of her.

I leaned in and kept my voice down, hoping to lead by example. "What do you mean exactly? What happened?" Though nothing made me angrier than scams targeted at seniors, I couldn't help but wonder if Mom might be partly to blame.

She wiped her eyes. "I tell you, I'm so mad. I want to kill that man!"

The rage in her voice pulsated through me. I sat rigid, wishing the table umbrella would shade me from more than the sun as I glanced around. I knew she hadn't meant that literally. But would others? With her hair dyed auburn to cover the gray, she could be my twin, albeit thirty years older. I touched the cross necklace I wore, not unlike hers, and hoped people wouldn't get us mixed up.

The way she exposed her problems to the world, laid her feelings out for perusal, shoved me to the limit. *My* bubble of personal space was more like a force field of stress-detecting sensors, similar to the United States military's measure of their defense condition readiness. And I was at DEFCON 3. My left eye began twitching.

A blond Swedish-looking couple having lunch at a nearby table eyed us. My best mind-your-own-business look produced the effect I wanted, or perhaps my nervous twitch gave me the appearance of a neurotic sociopath. They turned their attention to their plates as if suddenly fascinated by their food.

I positioned my Nikon to peer through the lens. During stressful moments this action became part of my relaxation technique. By transforming my camera into a crutch and looking through the lens, life narrowed down to manageable proportions, giving me a focused, clear perspective. *A safe perspective.* After a few wide-angle snapshots of the lake, which I could see well from my perch, I began to relax.

Only a few minutes before, Mom had found me taking pictures of the lake, which rested deep inside a volcanic caldera. The sides of the caldera made up the rim that dipped down two thousand feet before reaching the lake. The café seemed a good place to enjoy the beautiful seventy-degree weather and catch up with each other. I'd already had lunch as had Mom, so she'd ordered an iced tea. Now she had dropped the I-want-to-kill-someone bomb. All of a sudden this didn't seem like such a great place to discuss her problems.

"Why don't we go somewhere with more privacy?" I stood, glancing at the nosy couple. They remained devoted to their food. "Have you already checked in?"

Mom's eyes were as glassy as the lake. Had she even heard my suggestion? While I waited for a response, I studied her again. She'd never worn what I termed high fashion clothing but liked to dress in a matching theme from head to toe. Today's theme—penguins. Vibrantly colored sandals matched her slacks and shirt, embroidered with all manner of penguins. A missing penguin earring caught my attention. I should have realized right away that something was bothering her.

She tugged her earlobe and sniffled. "Oh dear, I've lost my earring." She slid her hand over the table as she searched then peeked underneath. "Ah, there it is." When her themed outfit was restored, she once again took up her demeanor of discontent. "I'm in room 325. Where are Rene and her fiancé? I thought you'd be with them."

"Rene is always late." I toyed with my camera, waiting for Mom to stand up. "She'll probably be late to her own wedding. Besides, I really don't expect them until later this afternoon."

I'd come to Caldera Lake National Park and the lodge where Rene, one of my longtime friends, was getting married on Sunday. We grew up in a nearby small town. The lodge was located in the Oregon Cascades, only a few hours' drive from the Oregon coast where I now lived, and only thirty minutes from where Mom lived. Rene had asked me to photograph the wedding. I'd been working too hard, was a wreck and grateful for the break. But I hadn't been there long enough for the fresh air to soften the circles under my eyes when Mom arrived, bearing her dreadful news.

She pushed to her feet, her frown making her look much older than her sixty-seven years. I paid for the tea while Mom leaned across her chair to retrieve her jean bag adorned with penguins. I shuddered at the thought of how much luggage she'd brought to maintain her themes.

"Polly! Is that you?" a voice asked from behind me.

I turned to see a man weaving his way around the tables toward me. He sported an awkward toupee. His strong cologne reached me before he did—something I never held in high regard. I sneezed three times, my normal response to strong scents.

Do I know him?

I tried to keep from frowning as my brain processed his appearance. He tugged his hand from his pocket and I thrust mine out, thinking he wanted to shake it. Instead, he brandished a bloodred handkerchief and blew his nose.

Ah. Now I remember.

"Alec?"

All the bitterness of the old grudge swept over me as I stared at this specter from my past: Alec Gordon. The memory of what he'd done still haunted me almost twenty years since last I saw him. Time didn't always heal old wounds. "What a surprise. What are you doing here?"

"I thought that was you." A tight-fitting maroon shirt revealed muscular arms and shoulders, with only a slight thickening at the waist.

At thirty-eight, I liked to consider myself healthy. But when

Alec looked me up and down, my cheeks grew warm. I thought to excuse myself and be done, but I couldn't be rude. Besides, Mom had created a scene moments before with her death threat. I hoped to be remembered only as a cameo, so I wasn't about to create another scene with Alec.

Unless my eyes played tricks, he appeared to push his chest forward, plumping himself up like a rooster. I didn't consider myself a spring chicken.

"I still live in the area. Own a big spread, too." He wiped his nose once more then stuffed the handkerchief back in his pocket. "I like to come up to Caldera Lake as often as I can. Fresh air and all that. I'm in real estate. How about yourself—what brings you here? I'd heard you'd gotten married and moved away."

When you meet someone from your school days, you want to show the portfolio of your success. Sharing the news with Alec that my husband went sailing eight years ago and never returned wasn't even at the bottom of my things-you-should-do-before-you-die list.

Never mind that during our high school years Alec had caused a tragedy that forever altered my life. I wasn't in the frame of mind to talk to him and didn't know what to say.

My mouth went dry as I floundered in a deep lake of resentment. I looked to Mom to throw me a life preserver.

She was gone.

My gaze ricocheted around the terrace in an unsuccessful search before returning to Alec. "Actually, I live in Gunner Beach and run a family portrait business. I have to admit, the beauty of Caldera Lake has me thinking about a different sort of photography."

Capturing the glorious scenery of the lake surrounded by mountains was just what my tired photographer's eyes needed. Though portraits were my primary source of income, the way people dressed for having their portrait done had taken its toll on me. One could only deal with so many pictures of mismatched jackets, earrings, and shoes. And pink lipstick made teeth appear yellow no matter how many whitening strips were used. Maybe my obsessive tendencies warranted therapy, but I resolved to avoid looking through critical glasses, at least for this long weekend.

"How long do you plan to be here?" Alec rocked back and forth on his feet.

His action reminded me of when I bought the boring four-door sedan I own. The salesman had done the same thing as he closed the deal and sold me a car I didn't want. I had the uncanny sensation Alec was about ready to close his deal. It made me nervous, because I wasn't for sale.

He apparently had no idea that I still held him responsible for the accident that killed my best friend in high school. Believing his next question would be about having dinner together, I took a step back, putting space between us. No sense giving him the wrong idea. The vibes he gave off made me think he knew I'd officially declared my husband dead last year.

"Actually, I'm here for a wedding and expecting my friends to arrive at any time. I'll be pretty busy for the next few days." There. That should take care of Alec Gordon. I'd been forceful yet gentle.

Alec looked disappointed, but I was relieved. This wasn't the place to drag up ghosts from the past, even if I'd been dragging one around with me for years.

He nodded, the space between his strawlike eyebrows shrinking as he frowned. "I understand. Well, maybe I'll see you around." He pulled a card from his pocket and gave it to me. "It was great to see you, Polly. You look terrific." Then he left.

Concerned over Mom's departure, I took off in the opposite direction from Alec and looked for her in the lobby. My cell phone was devoid of a signal, and Mom's probably fared no better. Not that it mattered, because Mom was one of those people who either forgot to carry her cell or forgot to charge it. She never checked her messages, claiming it was too complicated.

I rang her room from the lobby phone. After several rings and no answer, I hung up then searched the grounds without success. I knew what she was up to, because we'd done this many times before. She wanted me to imagine something had happened to her so that when I found her, I'd be so relieved I wouldn't be angry about whatever mess she'd gotten herself into. Well, I was in no frame of mind to play that game. She could find me when she tired of it. I returned to the lake rim to take more snapshots.

The lens needed adjusting to snatch photos of tourists as they stared at the water-filled caldera, their expressions betraying unspeakable awe. Capturing human life on film was in my blood, such that even the surrounding beauty couldn't completely pull me away. A short, thin woman wearing large, dark sunglasses leaned against the stone wall that bordered the drop of the rim. She turned in my direction and glared directly at me through my camera lens, or so it seemed. It unsettled me. I turned my attention back to nature.

After a full hour spent photographing the scenery and its inhabitants, the sense of accomplishment satisfied me. Before

Mom arrived, I'd e-mailed a few photos, along with a query letter about photographing national park historic lodges, to a magazine editor. Should she give me the assignment, I hoped to have plenty of pictures to work with. Eager to download the images to my computer and examine the fruits of my labor, I refused to give in to the nagging concern over Mom and headed to my room.

Surely the Royals would arrive soon—a reference I'd given to Rene and her fiancé, Conrad, as a joke, because he was British and looked like an older version of Prince William.

I was happy that she was finally getting married. I'd heard that a forty-year-old woman has a greater chance of being killed by a terrorist than finding love and getting married. I suspected those odds increased daily. Though not quite forty, Rene was fortunate to have beaten them. However, I believe it had more to do with trusting God than with fortune.

While strolling the hallway on the second floor, anxiety needled its way up my spine. This weekend would be a trial for me. I could feel it, as though I had a rare bone disease and a winter storm had blown in, exacerbating my symptoms. When I stood in front of the door to my room and reached for the knob, a woman's scream stopped my hand in midair. I froze, the sound curdling the contents of my stomach.

The screaming came from the room next to mine, and as abruptly as it started, it stopped. All manner of murderous images filled my mind. My knees turned to jelly. I took the few steps over to my neighbor's door and knocked gently. When that produced no answer, I pounded.

"Are you all right? Please, open the door. What's happened in there?" I jiggled the knob and pounded some more, begging for the screamer to let me in, while hoping I'd made a horrible mistake and someone simply had the television turned up too loud. The door opened slowly, sending fear and embarrassment through me.

But I had to know.

A red-haired woman appeared, her face stricken with terror. As she backed up, allowing me entrance, I recognized her uniform. She was one of the lodge housekeepers. I was hesitant about crossing the threshold, but then instinct took over, and I rushed to her side. "What happened?"

She pointed to the closet. I looked at the clothes on the hangers, then my gaze traveled to the floor.

A body lay on the mushroom gray carpet, looking like it had been shoved into the small closet.

Not just any body.

Alec Gordon's body.

CHAPTER TWO

I gasped.

"No! Alec!" I dropped to my knees and shook his lifeless form. His unresponsive eyes stared back. It was then that I saw the blood on the carpet and noticed more was crusted on the top of his head where his toupee should have been. Nausea gripped me.

I stood and moved away from him. There wasn't enough air in the room. I'd never been to DEFCON 2, but this had to be it. The reality of someone lying dead on the floor, someone I'd once wished dead, overwhelmed me.

I felt for my crutch, my fingers gripping the Nikon's cool surface. Camera in position, I took picture after picture, even turning the lens on the helpless woman before I realized how completely insensitive and rude I was being.

Horrified by the situation, by my own reaction to it, I sank to my knees as furious tears blurred my vision. I wanted to defend myself and admit to the woman that I'd only wished him dead in my friend's place, many years ago, but what would she think of me? Still, God knew the inner workings of my heart. And He knew this would happen. Had He allowed me to speak to Alec one last time? Had God given me the opportunity to forgive Alec and I'd failed?

A couple entered through the open door, wanting to know what had happened. I moved away from Alec so they could see for themselves. Though itching to start my photo frenzy again, I didn't want to feel like Lois Lane or some cheesy newspaper photographer. I tucked my camera behind me. Someone must have called the park rangers, because one finally appeared in the room, assessed the situation, then questioned us about how we found the body.

After taking my statement that I'd responded to the housekeeper's scream and seen the body in the closet, the park ranger released me with a warning that I would be called upon soon to give an official statement. I trudged down the hall away from the scene, away from my room, too stunned to do anything but drag one foot in front of the other. I felt like a zombie in one of those old black-and-white *Dialing for Dollars* monster flicks. The last few years, I had spent most of my evenings at home eating popcorn and watching movies with Murphy, my Jack Russell terrier. So my frame of reference relied heavily on movies.

Mom. I wanted Mom. Where was she? With a murderer on the loose, maybe I'd been wrong to ignore her disappearance. I hastened my way to her room on the third floor and pummeled the door.

"Mom, are you in there? Stop playing games with me. Something's happened." My voice cracked. "I need you." Then the tears came.

The door opened, and she appeared, arms wide. I went to her, breathing in the light scent of one of her knockoff perfumes, careful not to crush my camera between us.

"There, there. What's this all about?"

Relieved to find her safe in her room, I plopped onto the edge of one of the floral-covered beds, which smelled of lavender—too much lavender. The sneezes came as expected. After I wiped my eyes, I looked up at her then remembered her predicament. She stood haggard in a green velvet robe. Though in light of Alec's death—or his murder, given what I'd seen—her problems might be trivial, I wasn't sure that telling her about Alec was the best thing at the moment. I forced a smile to my face. She would find out soon enough.

"Sorry, Mom. It's nothing after all. It's just been. . .a hard week. Fortunately, I have Bridget to take care of the business for a few days."

"That flibbertigibbet?" Mom waved her hand, dismissing the idea that Bridget could handle things.

"Bridget may be scatterbrained, but she can hold down the fort for one extended weekend." Though Bridget had worked for me at Polly Perkins' Photography since its inception, I spoke with a confidence I didn't feel.

"How's Murphy?" she asked.

We'd now taken to discussing the mundane in order to avoid the urgent. "With Bridget." I knew what was next.

"Why didn't you bring him?" Mom examined her manicure, the action sending me back to parental interrogations from my childhood.

"I don't think he's allowed on the trails, for one." Nor did I want to split my support between a needy dog and the bride-to-be. "You can have him back if you want him." I didn't mean a word of that and held my breath.

"No, thank you." Mom dropped her nail inspection and went into the bathroom. I heard water gush from the faucet.

Mom had left Murphy with me five years ago, when she'd taken a cruise after her second husband died. She'd never taken Murphy back, and he'd since made a new home with me. He'd been named after Murphy's Law, because it wasn't long after she got him that everything that could go wrong, had.

In her mind anyway.

But, in the present case, he would have been better named after Murphy's Syndrome, if there were such a thing—multiple symptoms or events that formed an undesirable pattern—and it looked like Murphy didn't even have to be around for the syndrome to be in effect. Still, I missed him. I glanced at the phone, tempted to call Bridget to ask after him. Water stopped gushing in the bathroom sink, reminding me that I had more serious matters to deal with.

Mom came out of the bathroom and sighed when she plopped onto the other bed. I took a long breath and pushed back images of Alec's body. I needed to hear about Mom's problems first. Then I would decide how to tell her. She seemed so. . .fragile.

"Let's get back to our earlier discussion. Tell me what's happened to you. About the scam." I tried to soften my expression, letting her know that I loved her no matter what. It seemed funny, like I was the mother and she the child.

Mom moved to the window, pushing a curtain back to look out. "I'm sorry for abandoning you this morning. I just couldn't face that man."

My brows furrowed. "What man? Mom, please don't speak in riddles. Start from the beginning."

She turned to face me, her skin ashen. "It was that Alec Gordon. He's the real estate man who scammed me out of thousands." She put her hands to her face and sobbed. "Oh Polly, what am I going to do?"

Alec Gordon? My thoughts swarmed like bees in a beehive that had been sprayed with Raid. Utter chaos reigned. I even heard a loud buzzing noise in my head. "What? What are you talking about? You can't be serious." I grabbed her wrists, pulling her hands down. "Look me in the eyes, and tell me exactly what you mean."

Red-eyed, Mom stared at me as she spoke. "I gave your Alec Gordon fifty thousand dollars cash for a down payment on a real estate deal he brokered. It was meant to be an investment for the future. For *your* future. I don't think he remembered me from the funeral years ago. But I thought I could trust him because you knew him."

Fifty thousand dollars? Mom wasn't a wealthy woman, and I didn't even want to think about what her retirement fund looked like now. "First of all, he was never *my* Alec Gordon. And second, knowing someone does not equal trusting them." I couldn't suck in enough air and walked to the other end of the room, but, no surprise, there wasn't any more air there. After taking photos of Alec's body, holding my camera-crutch no longer held appeal.

I stood as tall as I could, expanding my lungs and gasping for air. Mom's sobbing grew louder, and she hadn't even heard the worst yet. She managed to dump prescription bottles out of a small paper bag then hand it to me.

Bag to my mouth, I sucked in a few breaths to minimize the hyperventilating. "Of course he remembers you. That's why it doesn't make sense. You don't scam someone you know. How could he get away with that?" He couldn't get away with it, and he didn't. It was obvious Mom hadn't been the only one he'd cheated.

"Well I'm sure I don't know, but he did."

The gravity of the situation hit me, draining all the energy from my body. How could I tell her about Alec? Suddenly gruesome images accosted me. Mom standing over Alec's body after. . . killing—no, I wouldn't go there. Yes, she'd had a motive. But probably so did plenty of other people. Yes, she'd been missing for hours. But that was only because I hadn't looked for her hard enough, right? But no matter how I tried, I couldn't argue away the morbid thoughts. Had Mom gone temporarily insane when she'd seen Alec?

I had no choice but to tell her. Swiping my hand over my face, I blurted the words. "There's something you should know."

Her expression made me think of a train barreling forward with no one in control. She had no idea what lay ahead but simply waited to hear how I would take care of her predicament—the small part of it that she knew. This was our pattern.

"So spit it out already." To Mom, patience was the British version of solitaire rather than a virtue to be practiced.

Patience notwithstanding, I wasn't sure that we weren't both pawns in someone's game, Mom a color-coordinated one, of course.

"Remember when you said you wanted to kill him?"

"Oh Polly, I wasn't thinking when I said that, even if he does deserve it. I haven't been sleeping well lately." She began stuffing the prescription bottles back into the sack. "And I don't think these new sleeping pills are helping either."

There was nothing for it. I had to tell her. "Someone killed Alec Gordon."

CHAPTER ‖ ‖‖ THREE

After Mom collapsed in hysterics, I convinced her to take a sleeping pill to calm her frenzied nerves. Though I wished I could do the same, it was early afternoon, and Rene was due to arrive soon.

I left Mom to sleep and wandered the halls again—this time in the sequel to the zombie movie. My mind floating somewhere between shock and apathy, I ended up in the lobby. I felt as if someone had Tasered me—stunned me with pain until I was numb. Despair settled on me as I thought about Mom's predicament. Of course, she was better off than Alec, but that thought did little to comfort me.

As I strolled around an area that probably spanned a good three thousand square feet, tourists poured through the doors, checking in or heading to their rooms or simply lounging on the great cushioned sofas. How did the authorities discover who killed someone when there were so many people milling about? There didn't appear to be any indication that a murder had taken place within the lodge. No stunned looks or wary whispering. Only jovial conversation and laughter pervaded the grand room. I assumed the hotel personnel would want the case settled as soon as possible.

Then it hit me. Random tourists would be of no more interest to the authorities than if the murder had been committed in a city filled with millions of people. Their first concern would be to locate and question those who knew Alec. The ranger had questioned me because I'd been in the room with the housekeeper, but I hadn't revealed that I knew Alec, because he'd never asked. Then there was Mom. Eventually someone would tell them about her outburst.

A deep breath cleared my thoughts, igniting my resolve. I needed to do everything I could to help Mom. I had to discover what I could about Alec's murder. It wasn't that I didn't trust the authorities.

"But. . .I *don't* trust the authorities." Had I said that out loud? Fingers pressed to my lips, I shrugged at a fifty-something woman who gave me a wary look.

She bent down to coddle her dog, a Jack Russell. Her actions made me miss Murphy. I could use the soothing effect of petting him right now.

I sighed and turned my thoughts to the unpleasant business at hand. I thought of how the news reported stories of people who'd been incarcerated for half their lives then released because of new evidence. I couldn't let that happen to Mom. I wasn't sure how to find the information, but foremost on my mind was to discover anyone else who Alec had cheated like Mom. Were they here today?

Not only did I have no clue about obtaining that sort of information, I had the added burden of making the necessary fuss over Rene—the bride-to-be—who would arrive soon. I plopped on a large, comfy-looking chair, sinking deep into the cushion. Getting out of the thing would be interesting.

While fidgeting with my camera, I mentally prepared to inform Rene about the murder. Telling her would cause a kaleidoscope of problems. She'd believe a murder at the lodge on the weekend of her wedding was a bad omen.

Even though she was now a Christian, Rene liked to hang on to old superstitions that her mother—who boasted involvement in a strange ancient religion I couldn't ever remember the name of—had taught her or made up if it suited her purpose.

As if my thoughts had conjured her, there Rene stood in the entryway to Caldera Lake Lodge. Always the nature girl, she looked as tan, trim, and fit as ever. She spotted me. We both screamed as we ran to each other and hugged. My heart beat with the joy of the reunion as well as the pain of the news I had for her. I held on to the hope that Alec's murder would not have a negative effect on Rene's wedding.

When she released me, I tugged at her ash-colored hair. The last time I'd seen her, she'd had a cropped, spiky look. But that had been three years ago. "You let it grow. It's so long."

"You like?" She primped and grinned, her face alight with happiness. "Oh Polly, it's wonderful to see you. Thank you so much for agreeing to this." She chattered on, working her words around her ever-present lozenge.

It was difficult to find an appropriate point at which to interrupt her ecstatic rambling but I managed. "Where's your sister?" Rene's sister, Veronica, was to be the matron of honor in this small gathering, which had me worried. Where Rene was always late, Ronni, as we called her, was always a no-show. Ronni was all that was left of Rene's family. Her parents were killed in a car accident years ago.

"She'll be along on Saturday. Don't you worry." She patted my shoulder.

"And Conrad?"

"He's getting the luggage. Should be right behind me." She jerked her head around.

Conrad strolled in on cue, looking tall and debonair.

I'd almost forgotten the heavy atmosphere I'd endured for the last couple of hours. But when a familiar silhouette appeared in the doorway and spoke to Conrad, my disquiet returned.

"Who's that with Conrad?" I asked. Recognition should have been instantaneous, but I clung to denial as if it were a lifeboat overturned by a troubled sea.

Rene slapped my arm. "Polly. Spence has agreed to be the best man."

Spence? My jaw dropped. *You call him Spence?* Shutting my mouth promptly, I eyed her, wondering if I would ever feel comfortable calling him Spence.

"Don't act so surprised. I'm sure I told you there was a possibility." An uncharacteristic giggle escaped her, though perhaps the excitement of the forthcoming wedding had simply caught in her throat. "The four of us together again. Isn't it wonderful? And Spence is still single." She winked.

Spencer Bradford III strolled into the lobby, accompanied by a gusty breeze, which mussed his sandy brown hair. He dropped one of the bags he carried and smoothed his hair back in place. A strange quiver worked its way up my legs. Why hadn't I anticipated that Spencer would come?

He'd lived next door to my father in London when I met him ten years ago. Rene had met Conrad while spending a summer with me there. We'd been a foursome, of sorts, but like so many other things in life, the fun didn't last. I never imagined I'd see him here. Apparently Conrad had grown very close to Spencer to name him the best man.

I glared at my friend. "I'm afraid you left off that little detail."

Rene huffed. "Surely you're not saying you wouldn't have come if you'd known he'd be here."

I suspected she'd hidden the fact from me because she was afraid of precisely that. Her frown only lasted a millisecond as Conrad caught her up in his arms and swung her around.

I made a mental sticky note to send my dog, Murphy, to the other side of the world, even though I knew that no distance would keep me from suffering from Murphy's Syndrome. I'd already been infected. Everything seemed to be tumbling into a series of unfortunate events, not to be confused with the actual children's book series, since I am neither an orphan nor do I possess a fortune.

Spencer, who stood a full head taller than Conrad, had dreamy blue eyes and was an older version of Westley from *The Princess Bride*, sans the black pirate gear. With his hands tucked safely in his pockets, he smiled at me from the other side of Rene and Conrad's embrace, though I sensed he was something other than thrilled to see me. Cautious perhaps—a sentiment I could well appreciate.

A feeling of déjà vu came over me. Here we were together again, approaching forty but still unmarried. This wasn't entirely true, if one counted my marriage to Brandon, even though he'd disappeared six months after we said our vows. But did that count if eight years later I'm still alone? And Conrad and Rene had made plans to wed several times but never made it to the altar.

Rene had commented how good it was for the four of us to be together again, but what a strange foursome we made.

The weekend at Caldera Lake that I had looked forward to as my breath of fresh air had turned stale with Alec's murder. Now with Spencer's arrival, I felt like I was smothering. This weekend, filled with marriage, murder, and mayhem, would be uncomfortable at best.

If things were to be salvaged, I had to start now. I stepped past Rene and Conrad, who were hugging like they hadn't seen each other in days. I knew how it felt to be that in love. Heat rushed up my neck. The very object of that memory stood before me. I glanced at Spencer, another man from my past.

God, what are you telling me?

"It's good to see you again." I realized when I said the words that I wasn't lying through my teeth. His blue eyes searched mine, looking for what, I wasn't sure. I had thought I never wanted to see him again. Spencer had been the love of my life. But he'd been unwilling to commit. Then Brandon had waltzed in and given me everything I'd wanted—commitment, marriage, a home.

Everything except love.

"How. . .how are you?" I loathed my faltering words.

A broad smile covered Spencer's tanned face. "Quite all right, Polly. And you?"

His British accent did crazy things to me. An ounce of hope wriggled through me that all would be forgiven and forgotten. A little yeast and all that. I missed his friendship. But allowing my thinking to take that path would quickly sour the moment, and I desperately needed to salvage this long weekend. For my sake, Mom's, and, though she didn't know it yet, for Rene's.

The image of Alec's body rushed through my mind, sucking the breath from me. My thoughts must have shown on my face, because Spencer stepped back, and I knew from his stricken look that he thought my sudden intake of breath was because of him.

Rene freed herself from Conrad and stood in front of me. "Polly, whatever is the matter?"

I took a deep breath. "Rene, Conrad. . .Spencer." I forced a weak smile when I looked his way. "There's something I need to tell you. Can we sit down?" I motioned to the overstuffed chairs near the fireplace. I was thankful the lobby had thinned out from a few minutes before, with people getting settled into their rooms or taking to the outdoors.

Rene paled as she sat next to me on the edge of a large ottoman. She dug through her purse then hastily unwrapped a lozenge and shoved it in her mouth. "Okay, give."

With all that was in me, I wanted to play this down so that the wedding could continue to be a joyous occasion. "I'm sorry if I alarmed you. I thought you should hear this from me. There was a tragedy in the lodge today."

Rene's eyes widened. "Oh no—"

"But it shouldn't affect your wedding," I added, hoping to stop her before she started. "One of the guests died."

Everyone except Rene appeared to relax. After all, death happened to everyone. Eventually.

Her left brow arched high, she leaned toward me and spoke in a slightly sardonic tone. "Died?"

I realized my mistake too late. Saying nothing would have been a better attempt to play things down. The fact that I'd even brought it up alerted Rene to the gravity of the situation. I swallowed and nodded.

"And just how did they die?" Ever the guarded cynic, Rene stood, challenging me.

Conrad was quick to follow and rubbed her arms while he cast a warning glance at me. "I'm sure this incident won't play any part in our big plans for this weekend." He turned her to face him and kissed her. "Right?" He tipped her chin to look up at him. "Rene?"

Conrad knew as well as I this occurrence could postpone the wedding.

Again.

The quicker I dispensed the news, the better. "A man was found dead in a closet earlier today. No one knows anything else." There. I'd told the truth, more like blurted, and managed to leave out the word "murder". . .and the small detail that I'd actually been involved in discovering the body. Still, I probably shouldn't have mentioned the closet.

"What?" Rene collapsed on the couch, her face as white as a wedding dress.

I looked to the others for help. Surely she didn't expect me to say it again. No one spoke as we stared at her. One wrong word could push her over the precipice of stability—a precipice upon which we all precariously braced ourselves. The woman held far too much power over the happiness of others.

"Don't you all see?" She thrust her hands out, pleading. "It's a very bad sign—an omen that can't be ignored. How can we possibly get married now?"

"Rene?" Conrad's voice teetered between fear and fury.

"Or ever. . ."

CHAPTER ⛩ FOUR

"No." The word rushed out like I'd collided with someone during a game of tag. My outburst occurred simultaneously with Spencer's. But our objections to Rene's suggestion didn't come close to hiding the strange sound that escaped from Conrad.

His expression contorted as he took a long breath. Perhaps he hoped to regain his composure, but he failed. A fierce huff forced its way from his nostrils. "You can't mean that, Rene. Not again."

He'd been through this with her before, so his strong reaction surprised me. I figured he should have expected it. Even better—prepared for it. I had always worried that his patience would come to an end long before they were married. Maybe he dared to hope the wedding plans would stick. But this time, he'd chosen the wrong adhesive—one that couldn't withstand a murder.

The memory of Alec's body made me shudder, drawing Spencer's attention from Conrad's histrionics. Though startled by the concern in Spencer's eyes, I shrugged off his attention, returning mine to Rene's response.

She gave none. Instead, she stared at the overlarge footstool in front of the couch as though the strange pattern provided the answers to the universe, or at least to her current dilemma. Her anguish appeared equal to that which she'd caused. Conrad turned his back to her and paced across the giant Persian rug, which seemed out of place in this rustic lodge. Animal skins were no longer politically correct. He stopped to stare at the fireplace, large enough for a man to stand inside, and thrust his hands through his hair.

I rushed to Rene, dropping to my knees beside the couch. Tears slid down her cheeks, and she squeezed her eyes shut, shaking her head as if in rhythm to a melody only she could hear—I imagined the theme song from *Out of Africa*.

I'd never been able to watch someone cry without joining them, but I wanted to encourage Rene, so I swiped at the tears on my face and composed myself. Still, I couldn't hide from the fact that I was to blame for the current scene in this tragic love story.

What had I done? Was it possible they could have enjoyed the weekend and completed their vows without hearing about Alec Gordon? Too late it occurred to me that the authorities probably wouldn't question my friends, because they hadn't arrived until after the murder.

Another tragedy could not occur on my watch. I wouldn't allow it. Sitting on the ottoman next to Rene, I whispered, "You two are meant for each other. This is absurd."

Conrad whirled to face me. I hadn't thought he'd heard me. Eyes aimed and mouth cocked, he readied to nail me with whatever form of ammunition he could muster.

"You." Rather than bellow, his voice came out in a venom laden snarl. "We would be married now if Rene hadn't insisted we include you."

I stood to face the one-man firing squad, believing that little Murphy should probably face it with me, because he was partly to blame. Everything that could go wrong had definitely gone wrong. "You mean. . . ." My words barely audible, I cleared my throat.

Conrad's eyes glistened. "I wanted to whisk her away this time—elope and honeymoon in the Swiss Alps. Instead of making plans that always seem to fall through. But she can't do anything spontaneous, and she insisted you be involved."

Conrad was impulsive, lived for the moment, and Rene tried to plan every moment in her day. I knew his venom only added to Rene's insecurities, her feelings that they were too different. But couldn't she see how much he loved her?

Rene stood then. "Would you two quit talking about me as though I weren't here? Besides, it's more than that and you know it, Conrad. I wanted us to marry here, where we first fell in love."

Conrad had been every hopeless romantic's dream when, years ago, he'd agreed to travel across the Atlantic to meet Rene at Caldera Lake—one of her favorite places—for a weekend of nature hiking and tree hugging. Rene loved all things primitive and organic and wanted to know if she had a future with the sophisticated and debonair Prince William look-alike.

Spencer placed his hand on my shoulder. "This isn't the time or place to discuss private matters. Let's register for our rooms, shall we?"

Conrad nodded. "Rene? Will you agree to stay so we can at

least talk this through?"

"Spencer's right. We need to talk about this in private." She glanced around the lobby.

Spencer gave my shoulder a quick squeeze, a vote of confidence that energized me. "No need for you ladies to move."

"I'll take care of the rooms, Rene." Frown lines remained chiseled in Conrad's face as he and Spencer headed to the registration desk. To have a man as handsome and doting as Conrad eager to escort her down the aisle—what must Rene be thinking to question marrying a guy like that? A twinge of jealousy stole through my heart. Not for Conrad, but for what Rene had with him and appeared to be throwing away.

I watched Spencer's tall, athletic form at the registration desk. I fancied that, in some way, Spencer's shoulder squeeze had been a protective gesture. My heart still warmed by the action, I shook my head. This wasn't the time for romantic giddiness.

I had to work fast. "Rene, I can't allow you to call off the wedding. I feel this whole thing is my fault."

She shook her head. "Polly, good grief. It's not your fault someone died in the lodge. So how can you blame yourself?"

What would she think if she heard the events of the morning—of Mom's involvement with Alec Gordon? "I'm thinking more along the lines that I shouldn't have told you. Maybe you never would have known, at least until after the wedding." That was pushing things, but considering Rene liked to spend so much time outdoors, maybe she would have escaped the news.

Rene sighed and plopped onto one of the sofas. She unwrapped another lozenge. At this rate, she'd run out of them before nightfall.

Finally she spoke. "Someone died here on the very weekend of our wedding. How can I ignore this omen?"

"No, listen to me. You're a Christian now. Why do you hold on to ridiculous superstitions?" A quick glance to the registration desk rewarded me with a wink from Spencer. He'd known I would talk to Rene.

Rene looked at me, her eyes slowly focusing, as though shedding blinders. "I know you're right."

"You need to read your Bible and pray. Get some rest. That will clear your head, and you'll be as good as new."

A weak smile curved her lips. "You're good to me, Polly. I wish I could believe you. "

"It's just wedding jitters. You should know that by now."

They'd been close to their wedding day three times now. Though stable was not a word used to define their relationship, I knew they belonged together. If only Rene could overcome the fear that kept them apart.

"We're checked in." Conrad frowned at me as he took Rene into his arms. Her resistance appeared to melt as he rubbed his hand down her back, like someone who cherished a priceless possession.

They would be fine.

I looked to the fireplace, the chairs, other tourists, anything but their private moment. Spencer stood uncomfortably near as memories of tender moments accosted me. I risked a glance at him. He looked rigid and strained, but gentleness dwelled in his eyes. Was he remembering as well?

I couldn't breathe and paced the cozy area encompassing the rug.

Conrad and Rene walked away arm in arm. "See you for dinner, Polly," she called over her shoulder.

I hoped she'd remember our discussion and that she'd marry Conrad this time. Unsure if my legs would carry me anywhere, I slumped onto the sofa to gather my bearings.

I was thankful when Spencer sat across from me, not next to me. "Spot on, Polly. What did you say to her?"

"Just reminded her that she's a Christian. Forget the superstitions." I rubbed my temples.

"Right you are. I knew you could straighten this whole misunderstanding out. You were, after all, always straight to the point."

I'd closed my eyes momentarily, but they popped open as I frantically tried to read between the lines of his statement. Was he referring to my need for a commitment from him during the time we'd been a couple?

He quirked a half smile, and I feared he could read my mind. "I meant that as a compliment, Polly."

I laughed. "So you *were* reading my mind."

"Not exactly. I just know that you apply multiple meanings to simple statements."

I frowned then realized I was doing it again. "Listen. . . ."

"You look as though you could use some rest. And I know that I could. It's been a long day."

"I'm sorry for keeping you. I forgot all about your travels."

Spencer stood up and so did I. He closed the small distance between us, coming much too close for comfort.

He leaned in. With stomach clenched and heart pounding, I braced myself. Would he kiss me? His quick peck on my cheek answered my nervous question. He left me reeling in the scent of his cologne. I touched my face where his lips had been.

No, no, no. . .

Now wasn't the time for my brain to go all fuzzy, thinking about this unnerving man who invoked any number of pleasant memories—along with unpleasant ones.

Confused and drained after coming face-to-face with two men from my past—one hated, one loved—and the accompanying memories, I felt like a character in some sort of twisted spoof of *A Christmas Carol.*

As if in answer to my thoughts, somber figures entered the lobby, wheeling a body covered with a dark sheet.

—

"Oh bother." Mom dug through her purse as we waited for the slow-moving elevator to edge its way from the third floor to the first. "I forgot to take an ibuprofen. I must have left the bottle in my room." She snapped the bag closed and looked at me, an apology in her eyes.

"Oh no you don't." I pursed my lips, standing my ground. She wasn't going to get away with using something like ibuprofen as an excuse to miss dinner. "The last thing you need is to be alone right now. You'll only get more depressed."

Not to mention staying hidden might translate into her perceived guilt. I smiled to disguise my concern. Then my nose crinkled. I wasn't sure if the stale cigarette smell came from the elevator or from Mom. The doors of the elevator weren't in any more of a hurry than the elevator. I followed her out of the contraption into the hallway, catching a whiff of *au de cigarette* from her clothing.

"Mom, have you started smoking again?"

She jerked her head back and gave me a quizzical, indignant look. "I haven't touched those things in five years. You know that."

"Really?" I wanted to believe her, to push my doubts aside.

She looked up and down the long hall, tugging at her bottom lip. At first I thought she would brush aside my question. Then suddenly she yanked her purse open and grappled with a pack of cigarettes. She thrust them in my face as she squeezed, broken white sticks tumbling to the floor. "Is this what you want to see? Well, I'm sorry. I couldn't help it. This thing with Alec. . .it has me frazzled."

"Shh. Do you want someone to hear you?" Mom was a nervous wreck. I said nothing more but sent up a silent prayer as I bent over to pick up the mess she'd made. I stuffed the broken cigarettes in a nearby trash receptacle. *Lord, please let this be over soon.*

I was afraid of what this weekend would end up doing to all of us. The lodge had moved me to a room away from the crime scene because I'd asked, but I suspected the rangers would have made the request themselves, due to the investigation. I had to repack my bags and change rooms then hurriedly get ready for dinner. They hadn't moved me any closer to Mom though. I remained on the second floor, she on the third.

When I went to get her for supper, we'd discussed Alec's death. I told her all about Rene's reaction and that the wedding plans were on unsteady ground. The thought struck me that they were on unsteady ground literally as well as figuratively. Caldera Lake was still considered an active volcano, though it hadn't erupted in. . .hundreds of years? I wasn't sure.

"I can feel a migraine coming on. I really should go back for some ibuprofen."

"You just need something to eat. Being around other people will help you relax." I tugged at her elbow.

She didn't budge.

"Mom, all we have to do is smile and discuss everything good, praiseworthy, and beautiful at dinner. However that verse goes."

"Oh, all right. But if my head starts that horrible pounding, I'm leaving."

We headed down the hallway toward the restaurant. Slow, steady breaths helped to calm my rising anxiety. Practicing one's own advice was a lot more difficult than dishing it out. Rene had phoned an hour earlier to confirm we'd all meet for dinner. Though she sounded rested—and there was the usual singsong to her voice—her tune rang flat. She hadn't made her decision yet, I could tell. I hoped we could all enjoy dinner and, at least for the time, forget about murder and wedding plans gone wrong. Though I couldn't force the others to agree to my way of thinking, I resolved, for my own peace of mind, to think about only good things. Well, except for one. I wouldn't think about the feelings and memories Spencer's presence stirred in me.

The Caldera Lake Dining Room stood before us—fine dining featuring Northwest cuisine. We stepped through the doors to the muted sounds of diners and clinking dishes. I spotted Rene and Conrad, and the hostess led us to their table. They shared greetings with Mom as we sat at the table, which was covered with white lace over a green tablecloth.

But where was Spencer? I might give the wrong impression if I asked after his whereabouts.

Rene pulled a bag of lozenges out of her purse. After unwrapping one and popping it into her mouth, she and Conrad loosely held hands on the table. He toyed with Rene's pinky finger. She attempted conversation with Mom around the lozenge, but it was easy to see they were both preoccupied, and even I had to feign interest. Rene's smile seemed limp, and the shadows beneath her eyes told where her thoughts were.

I'd resolved not to think about Spencer, but what choice did I have? It was either Spencer or Alec Gordon. Spencer's absence screamed for my attention. I conjured up all sorts of imaginings: I'd spoken to Alec Gordon, a man from my past, who ended up dead. Spencer was also a man from my past, and, though I knew little about fast cars, my imagination shifted into high gear. I wished I'd never watched all those Alfred Hitchcock movies.

A deep sigh escaped. It felt as if I'd released all my depressing thoughts in one breath. Horrified, I recovered with a quick smile.

"What's wrong?" Rene asked. She looked expectant, like she thought I'd made an important discovery. Was she pretending that she'd forgotten about the death?

"Nothing." Still, thoughts of Alfred Hitchcock disturbed me, because he was another dead man. Where was Spencer?

The glass of water I'd been tapping fell over, due to one tap too hard, and soaked the tablecloth. I scooted back to avoid getting water on my favorite turquoise-colored slacks.

"Oh, Polly." Mom's expression teetered between agitation and concern as Rene and I worked to clear the mess.

I was thankful Mom didn't bring up the obvious. She knew it was best not to unwrap what we'd neatly wrapped and topped with a bow in our agreement to discuss only the good. Though I didn't remember if Mom had actually agreed.

A twentysomething waiter came to assist with extra napkins then took our drink orders. He smiled and thanked us before moving from the table, revealing Spencer standing behind him.

Spencer caught the waiter's attention before he'd moved too far and gave his order. Tomato juice with lime. His tastes hadn't changed much. I wondered if his tastes in women had. He pulled out the chair directly across from me and winked as he sat. Not wanting to appear like a giddy schoolgirl, I offered a weak smile.

But a giddy schoolgirl was exactly what I felt like. Ridiculous.

He unbuttoned his sports jacket, looking resplendent. I suppose that's what first attracted me to him all those years ago. His gaze flicked from his menu to me. Mine flitted back to my own menu in search of my usual dish. But food wasn't the only thing on my mind. The waiter brought our drinks and took our orders.

Spencer struck up a lively conversation. It had always been his nature to relax people. I was glad he noticed our dire need. Soon we were all mesmerized, lost in the hypnotic effect his voice created.

The conversation went from rare breeds of dogs to the race to claim the Arctic. I'd never realized the Arctic hadn't been claimed yet. Apparently with the melting of the polar ice cap, the battle was on. Perhaps Spencer's delay to dinner could be blamed on whatever magazine he'd browsed before coming down. In any event, he discussed countless topics to lighten the mood.

When the discussion turned to what each of us had been doing over the past few years, I excused myself and went to the ladies' room. I didn't want to share how drab my life had been after Brandon's disappearance. Or how my thoughts had turned to Spencer and all the unanswered what-ifs of our long-ago relationship. What was I thinking? Spencer had his chance with me. He'd been unwilling to step into a more serious commitment. And I was too old to play those games now. I wouldn't make that mistake again.

I exited the bathroom stall. "Like he's even expressed an interest in me." I thrust my hands under the running faucet then gave a brief smile to a woman washing her hands.

"Excuse me?" She eyed me curiously.

Had I said that out loud? "I'm sorry. . .it's nothing." I tried to hide my embarrassment and focused on lathering the soap on my hands. But I so wanted to stare at her. In that short glimpse, she'd caught my photographer's eye.

In the mirror, I noticed her shrug. She turned her back to put her hands under the dryer. That was my chance. I continued to wash my hands and stared at her reflection. She looked like a grown-up version of Emily the Strange, at least what I imagined Emily the Strange would look like if she were a real person. In actuality, Emily the Strange was a brand name of preadolescent, gothic-themed products.

Facing the mirror, she inspected herself. Long black hair down to her midback, green eyes peered from beneath her bangs. Skulls and black cats decorated her clothes. Mom would have had a fit to see that her elegant earrings didn't match her clothes.

I'd long forgotten not to stare when she flashed a you-must-be-crazy look at me then spun on her heel and left.

When I returned to the table, our food had arrived, and Spencer was deep in conversation with Conrad. I sat down to my usual Hawaiian chicken with rice pilaf. The rest of us were quiet, as though we were too busy eating the wonderful fare to talk. I noticed I wasn't the only one pushing food around my plate. We'd hoped to enjoy our evening and forget about what had happened earlier this afternoon. As I gazed around the dining room at other diners, I couldn't help but wonder if they were pushing food around on their plates as well. Had they heard the murderous news by now?

If so, how could they eat at such a time? For that matter, how could I? Everyone was going about their lives as if nothing had happened. A chilling thought hit me. Any one of the diners could be the murderer. We could be dining with a killer. The girl in the restroom could even be the killer. I dropped my fork.

Spencer drew his gaze from Conrad. "Polly, you look like you've seen a—"

Rene choked on her water and began coughing uncontrollably. Mom patted her on the back. Why did people always think that helped? Rene lifted her giant purse onto the table as though it held a twenty-pound weight. On the positive side, we could use it for a weapon if needed.

She began scrambling through the contents—a nervous habit not unlike Mom's. She dumped everything onto the table, surprising us all. Rene had always carried a pharmacy in her purse, and tonight was no exception. Analgesics, nose spray, prescription bottles, and of course, the lozenges. The irony in light of her granola bar ideology wasn't lost on me. She quickly snapped up her inhaler.

I recalled the first time I met Rene. I was thirteen and had just learned my parents were divorcing. I had escaped to a nearby park to cry out my frustration and sorrow, and Rene found me, sitting in a swing, weeping and gasping for breath. I couldn't get enough air. Rene came to my aide, offering her inhaler—though I didn't have asthma. Our similar reactions to the stresses of life brought us together, resulting in a lifelong friendship. I would have smiled at the memory, but Rene was suffering at the moment.

After two puffs, she held her breath.

I think we all did.

Finally Rene leaned back in her chair, releasing her breath. She blinked rapidly, put a broad smile on her face, and started cramming everything back into her purse. "So Polly, how's the photography business? Bridget? That dog. . .what's his name?" Of course, she wanted to divert the attention away from herself and, I suppose, onto me, because I'd been absent during their show-and-tell of the past.

"Yes, Polly. Let's hear about that dog of yours. It's Murphy, if I'm correct." Spencer grinned, obviously lending his help to lighten the conversation.

My heart skipped. How would Spencer know about Murphy unless Rene had told him? Did that mean he'd asked about me? They'd been discussing me? "Yes, it's Murphy. Remember. . . after the law? To tell you the truth, he's been a problem lately. Growling and baring his little teeth—cantankerous as ever." Though I knew the conversation would grow lighter if we talked about the weather, I enjoyed sharing about Murphy, and that embarrassed me. I rather missed him. For a moment, I pictured him dressed in a little black jacket with a bow tie, sitting at the table with us. The image brought a smile to my lips.

But Rene didn't seem to share my vision. She dropped her

fork. That made two fork droppings at the table tonight. Her eyes grew wide as she stared behind me. Spencer looked stricken. Earlier Conrad had given his roll to Spencer because he was on a starch-free diet—or "lifestyle", as he called it—but now he snatched the roll back and began buttering it. He appeared to have every intention of eating it.

"Whatever is the matter?" Mom turned to see and gasped.

Other diners casually glanced in the same direction, but their reactions weren't as severe. My back was to the door, so I scooted my chair enough to see what had caused the commotion.

Three park rangers stood in the restaurant entrance.

CHAPTER FIVE

Unfortunately the diners at my table were all guilty by reaction.

Except for one thing—of our little wedding party, only Mom and I were at the lodge when Alec was murdered. Spencer, Rene, and Conrad hadn't yet arrived. It seemed odd that the appearance of rangers in the restaurant should have such a dramatic effect on Spencer and Conrad. Then again, their apprehension could be centered around Rene's possible overreaction.

Dressed in typical national park garb, the rangers filed into the room, removed their ranger hats, and quietly dispersed among the various tables of diners. One of them—the tall, nice-looking one who had been first on the scene of the crime—strode directly to our table.

He addressed us with his hands behind his back. "Good evening. I'm sorry for interrupting your dinner. I'm Park Ranger Jennings." A nod to the badge he wore confirmed this for us, as if we wouldn't take his word.

"What's this all about?" Spencer was quick to the point, though he'd earlier pinned that description on me.

Ranger Jennings looked at me, recognition registering on his face. "As some of you may already know, there's been a death in the lodge. Preliminary findings suggest we're dealing with a homicide. We've secured the crime scene and are gathering forensic evidence."

Rene sucked in a breath, but I stared straight ahead, vaguely aware that everyone sat stiff, waiting to hear the rest.

Ranger Jennings paused, allowing us to absorb this information before he continued. "We're asking all the guests to remain at the lodge until we've interviewed them."

"But how long will that take? What if we need to leave? This is ridiculous." Spencer tossed his napkin on the table and leaned back, cocking his head just so. A challenge, to be sure.

"If you need to leave, please check with us first." Ranger Jennings continued, dismissing Spencer as though he'd not heard a word. "On the other hand, if we consider you a suspect. . . " He didn't bother to finish his statement. Instead, he eyeballed everyone at the table to make sure we understood, his gaze stopping to rest on Spencer.

"I'm not up on American law, but I do watch the American version of *CSI*—you can't keep us without a reason." Spencer arched his brow.

What was he doing? I kicked him under the table.

"Ouch." Rene jumped in her seat and glared at me. I mouthed an apology.

Ranger Jennings's smile flattened. I imagined that he wanted to do more than lose his smile. I had to admire him for keeping his composure. "The state police detectives will help us with the initial investigation until such time as we, the U.S. Park

Service, have adequate resources in place. With scores of tourists to interview, we ask for your patience. And sir—" Ranger Jennings took his turn at arching his brow as he singled out Spencer "—we rely on tried-and-true methods of investigation."

Oh great! What exactly did that mean? The old-fashioned way? I glanced at Mom, remembering our earlier conversation. "Pale" wasn't a strong enough word to describe her.

Ranger Jennings pulled out a notepad and pen. "Can I get your name, sir?"

Spencer's mouth dropped open. "Now wait just a minute—"

"Sir?"

Conrad nudged Spencer into compliance. I'd never seen him so cheeky, to put it in his words. Why wasn't he cooperating? His attitude seemed to draw the ranger's attention.

"Spencer Bradford." Elbow on the table, he covered his mouth and looked away, clearly disgruntled.

"Thank you. Now, if I could get all of your names, this will help me keep tabs on who I've informed."

My lungs ached. In fact, they'd deflated.

I feared that Spencer had crossed some sort of invisible line with the ranger—the one that authorities use to determine who they'll ask nicely and who they'll force into submission. I resolved to be on the compliant side—I needed all the help I could get. And so did Mom.

Ranger Jennings continued to glance at Spencer with the slightest of scowls while writing down each of our names. I hoped he noted he'd already interviewed me once. Queasiness threatened at the thought of Alec's corpse. I looked down at my plate and wondered if the ranger planned to reimburse us for the dinner he'd spoiled.

My spirits dipped even lower when Mom gave her name. I had to keep reminding myself that she wasn't guilty. But why did I have to work so hard to believe it? Ranger Jennings nodded when he finished and told us he'd be in contact soon.

He left us sitting in silence. I stared at my plate until Rene's sniffles became too urgent to ignore. I looked up and was stunned to find her staring at me, her expression cross.

"This whole time you've known this was a murder, haven't you? Why weren't you up-front with me?" Rene tossed her napkin to the table and ran from the room.

Conrad scooted his chair back and called after her. "Rene. . ." He looked at me as he stood. "Well, this is just great." He left in pursuit.

Why was everyone blaming me? I looked from Spencer to Mom, expecting an answer to my unspoken question. Though they'd not voiced an opinion, I assumed we'd all agreed to shelter Rene from the truth for as long as possible.

Mom stood. "Polly, sorry, dear, but my head is killing me." She gathered her purse. I don't think she noticed her unintended pun. I watched her until she disappeared through the exit, leaving me. . . .

Alone with Spencer.

The waiter brought our desserts and discovered that more than half the table had gone.

"If you don't mind, we'll eat our dessert, and you can return the others. Sorry, chap." Spencer gave me his half-dimpled smile.

My heart rate kicked up a notch. On the edge of my mind, I could sense my anxiety rising. Without my camera, I had no hope of controlling it. Migraines were like that. Somewhere in my head I would feel the smallest of throbs, and I knew if I didn't control it soon with an analgesic, it would take over. But I had no drug for what troubled me now. I tried to conjure Murphy in his tuxedo again to relax but couldn't even remember what he looked like. Did he have a dark patch on one eye or both?

"I'm not sure I can eat now. Everything is just so. . .awful." I stared at the Black Tuxedo Cheesecake on my plate. In my peripheral vision, I could see the rangers approaching tables to share the news. What made me think I could discover the killer on my own?

"On the contrary, Polly. I've never known you to turn down cheesecake, and I believe the occasion warrants indulgence."

Spencer's cell rang to the hip-hop tune of "I've Got the Power." The song surprised me because it was a little brazen for his tastes, not to mention the fact he actually had cell service—something I'd not managed to achieve since arriving.

He answered then shoved it at me. "For you."

I mouthed "me?" and took it from him. "This is Polly."

"You're going to have to talk some sense into her," Conrad said. I moved the phone from my ear, feeling as if his growl would include a bite or at least a nip.

After bringing it close again, I answered. "Okay. . .um, I'll be right there."

Spencer stabbed a fork into a piece of his strawberry cake, looking like he'd accepted his fate on a sinking *Titanic*.

I scooted from the table. Rene and Conrad's troubles were one thing, but Mom would become a person of interest if the rangers discovered her relationship with Alec and her outburst at the Terrace Café. As I looked at the man from my past sitting across from me, I considered that I might not come through this unscathed—I, too, had a relationship with Alec Gordon. Would the authorities discover my hidden ill will toward him?

I could only manage a wan smile as I bade Spencer good evening.

———

"But Polly, how can you believe we should continue forward with our wedding plans? Even if we did, even if it weren't a bad omen, how could I ever forget this. . .this horrible weekend?" Rene broke into tears, her sob-speak tumbling out. "Our wedding should be the memory of a lifetime."

I put my arms around my friend and soothed her with words of encouragement, much like Mom had done earlier today for me. Rene was right, of course. If they'd been allowed to go about their lives, forgetting about Alec Gordon, then maybe the wedding wouldn't become soiled with the murder. I wanted to say that if I loved a man like she loved Conrad, I wouldn't allow anything to get in the way of marrying him. But I knew that comment would draw a sympathetic look from Rene, since she'd always believed Spencer and I were meant to be together.

Instead I said, "I don't have the answers. But I do know that if we pray about this and earnestly seek God's leading, we'll have our answer."

An inward pang, spiritual in nature, caused me to squeeze my eyes shut. Once again I was dishing out advice that I struggled to follow myself. When I opened my eyes, Rene had closed hers, believing I'd been in prayer. I bowed my head and focused my heart on God, knowing that words spoken out loud affected nothing if they weren't from the heart.

"Lord, I pray for your direction and guidance in this situation." I continued for a while, praying for Rene, Conrad, Mom, and the whole murder investigation then paused to allow Rene her words. When our prayers were spent, a gentle, holy peace settled upon me. I looked at Rene and saw she felt it, too. We wiped the tears and hugged.

"I must look a mess," she said, looking intently at me.

"By the expression on your face, I'm guessing that I'm the one who looks a mess."

Rene giggled. "Do you remember the time you were putting together that huge casserole for a potluck?"

I stared at the ceiling as if the memory would replay itself like a movie on the white surface.

"Don't you remember? Conrad and Spence had arrived early to escort us to the bash. You turned just as Conrad came up on you from behind."

An image of Conrad covered with tomato sauce and noodles appeared in my mind. "The look on his face."

Rene's laugh was contagious, and I joined in, relieved, believing she'd overcome all her misgivings.

"Priceless." We said the word together and laughed hysterically like two young girls who'd become slaphappy over rum punch.

When the laughter died, we were wiping tears of joy.

"I've come to a decision," Rene said.

I could hope, pray, and lead a woman to a wedding, but I couldn't make her say vows. I held my breath.

"My wedding can still be a wonderful, memorable occasion, despite all these nasty interruptions. Besides, I want to begin making memories with Conrad. . .as his wife."

I screamed, and we both jumped up and down. She'd finally come to terms with what had kept her from marrying Conrad—the postponements, the cancellations for trivial reasons—and she would marry the man. I knew it was true. And I knew she couldn't wait to tell Conrad the news.

The clock revealed it was after midnight. "I can't believe we've been talking for so long. I'd better let you get some sleep."

Rene smiled. "Thank you, Polly. Conrad didn't understand how much I needed you. But I think he will now."

I thought he would, too, and maybe he would even thank me. "Well, what about Conrad? Will you tell him tonight?"

Rene looked at the clock again then the phone. "I'll call him—keep a little tension and romance in the relationship."

I left Rene to her phone call and returned to my concern for Mom. But there wasn't any way I'd disturb her at this late hour and risk waking her. She'd probably taken another sleeping pill. I was wide awake, my mind filled with thoughts of how to discover Alec's killer.

Though I knew I should return to my room, I headed for the lobby. I'd always wondered about the giant fireplace there. Caldera Lake Lodge rested at over eight thousand feet above sea level, so even the summer nights were cold. Did they keep the flames stoked during the night or allow the fire to die down? My detour would only take a few minutes.

The lobby was quiet except for the crackle of flames. The ambience created by the gentle fire warming and dimly lighting the room caused imaginings of a different life to bubble up. Pleasant feelings engulfed me, and I allowed myself, if only for a moment, to think about what life might have been like had my husband stayed home on that fateful day. Or what life might have been like had Spencer. . . I jammed my hands into my pockets, killing that thought.

It was one thing for Rene and Conrad to continue with wedding plans, but it was quite another for me to entertain romantic notions about a man who, as far as I was concerned, had spurned me years before.

I had to get serious about my investigation into Alec's death. With that thought, it occurred to me how careless I'd been. Someone had murdered Alec Gordon, and here I was, meandering around in the middle of the night by myself. It wasn't smart or safe. But the rangers hadn't issued any warnings or closed down the hotel, so perhaps they believed only Alec Gordon had been the target. I chose to take the high road of thinking the rest of us were safe. For now.

The cozy, overstuffed chairs, soaked in firelight, called to me. I strolled toward one of them. Two tall chairs faced the fire at an angle, and I approached from behind. A hand unexpectedly dropped from the arm of the chair.

I froze.

Why had I thought I'd be the only one here? Could it be the killer? I took quiet steps until I could see who'd disturbed my own private sitting room.

Spencer!

He'd been part of my imaginings, and there he sat, in the flesh. Something serious had happened, Rene was getting married, and

I needed all my faculties about me. Spencer's presence didn't suit my purposes. I took one step back, thinking to return to my room before he spotted me.

My, but he was handsome.

A sigh escaped.

Did I do that? Had he heard me?

His head jerked around. "Ah. . .Polly. You couldn't sleep either? Or. . .have you been with Rene all this time?"

I nodded and smiled. "I think the wedding is on again."

"Yes, but for how long?" He rubbed his chin. Even in the low light, I could see the shadow of stubble.

"You know, I think it's going to last this time." I approached the fire to rub my hands. Spencer came to stand beside me. This cozy, romantic atmosphere was probably the worst place for me to be with the man. I had to get a handle on my decade-old feelings for him. He wasn't the same person I'd known before. I wasn't the same person.

"I hope you're right. For our sakes as well," he said.

We stood side by side, staring at the fire. Once the warmth became too much, I rubbed my neck, thinking I needed to head to bed.

Spencer must have sensed my intentions. He'd always been good at that. "I know it's late, Polly, but I was hoping we'd have some time to talk." He motioned for me to sit.

A nervous laugh escaped me. "No time like the present." I plopped into a chair, feeling tired yet enlivened all the same. I could listen to Spencer's accent for the rest of the night. Or forever.

Spencer shared delightful tales of his travels to Thailand and other exotic countries. Though I'd not wanted to speak of my past at dinner, his easy ways brought out things long left unsaid. He sounded sincerely sorry when I told him about Brandon's disappearance. Though sitting with him and reminiscing warmed my heart, at the same time, a sense of dread chased me. All this talk of things gone wrong. I should have learned something by this time.

Spencer pushed deeper into his chair. "Whatever happened to us, Polly?"

I dared to glance at him, afraid my eyes would reveal what I'd not even figured out. *You couldn't commit to me.* "It was so long ago."

"Yes, but I've missed you. I can't for the life of me figure out why I let you—"

"Stop. . . !" I stood and faced him. "There's no need to go back. We're here for mutual friends. I hope we can remain on friendly terms as well. It's been nice discussing the past with you—"

"But?" Spencer raised his left brow.

How could I tell him I didn't want to get hurt again, that I feared I was already there? I couldn't form the words, as if my mouth were full of crackers—the white-flour, trans fat kind.

"Before you go, I have a. . .a confession of sorts."

Exhaustion began to overwhelm me. Finally. "Is it really necessary? I'm not sure there's anything you need to confess." I said the words, yet I sat again and waited.

"The truth is, I arrived here yesterday—a full day before Rene and Conrad."

What was he trying to say? "Travel to a remote location is hard to manage sometimes. You don't always arrive when you want to."

"Polly, that's not it. I was anxious to see you after all these years. I hoped to catch you before the others arrived."

Air rushed from my lungs. Probably not the reaction he'd hoped for. I'd spent the day fighting off nuances of romance with him, feeling safe in my belief that we'd both moved on, that he wasn't interested in me.

But now this.

He'd hurt me. *Hang on to that thought. Remember the pain.*

Spencer scooted to the edge of his chair and rested his elbows on his knees. "I saw you this morning, on the terrace."

Terrace? Alec Gordon was on the terrace, too. I stiffened.

He shook his head, reading my thoughts again. "I saw you with *him*."

"I can explain." What was the matter with me? I sounded frightened, like I was guilty.

"I'm afraid I'm the one who needs to explain. I had no right. I know that now. But when I saw the man return to the terrace after your brief encounter with him, I approached him and started a conversation. He told me he was in real estate and gave me his card. I hoped to find out if you were in a relationship with him, or what, if any, was his interest in you."

All too familiar with the jealous side of Spencer, heat rose in my chest. "You what?"

"I'm apologizing now. I had no right."

"None."

"I couldn't possibly repeat his words to you, but he revealed himself to be a cad in the most distasteful way. He isn't good enough for you."

Protection, Spencer? The thought kindled a warm fire inside, but I reminded myself that it came a decade too late. I sat in stunned silence.

"There was a nasty confrontation in which I warned him to stay away from you. How was I to know he'd end up dead hours later?"

"You couldn't have known that any more than. . ." I pressed my lips together, unwilling to share Mom's predicament. As far as the terrace crowd was concerned—at least those who were interested in others' affairs—Alec had one person who'd wanted him dead and another who'd given him a stern warning. Both of these people were close to me.

"What else did you say?"

"I told him to stay away from you. . .or else."

CHAPTER SIX

I told him to stay away from you. . .or else.

Spencer's words from the night before stirred me awake. Bright sunlight beamed through a slit in the heavy drapery. A lighted 7:00 stared back at me from the digital clock. So much for sleeping late. I should ask for a room on the west side. I stretched. Actually, I probably should have shared a room with Mom so I wouldn't have to worry about her. Maybe then she wouldn't have been tempted to smoke. Either that or I would have suffered with the stench and struggled to breathe.

I wasn't sure how I felt about what Spencer had said to Alec. As Spencer had so kindly reminded me, I had a way of overanalyzing things. Was he just being a protective big brother or friend? Or had he been impulsive and revealed his feelings for me, not wanting anyone else to have me?

"Yeah, right!" I sat up in the bed and scratched my head. I needed to check on Mom.

The phone rang as I reached for it. She was probably calling me first. "Mom?"

"What? No, this is Rene." Her words were shaky. She blew her nose to make sure I knew she'd been crying. It was her way.

What now? After last night's prayer with her, I hoped we weren't back on her roller coaster of emotions.

"What's happened?" I extended the cord as far as it would go, but it didn't reach the bathroom. I settled for examining my haggard appearance in the dresser mirror.

"The rangers are interviewing Spencer."

I took a deep breath. "Yes, well, they're interviewing everyone." *Right?* There wasn't any reason to worry.

"It's more than that. Conrad's here in my room. He said that someone reported that Spencer had a confrontation with Alec."

"How. . .how do you know that?"

"Conrad was with him this morning for an early breakfast. They took Spencer to someplace private for questioning. Conrad said they had a serious interest in him. He was a special person of something. "

"Interest. A person of interest." I'd heard the term often enough over the years on the news stations I watched.

"I thought you should know. So what are your plans for this morning?" She'd moved on from her sniffle-nosed concern for Spencer. Yep, we were back on the roller coaster. But who was I to judge? Getting married might put me on an emotional edge as well. Perhaps she was more like Mom than I thought, though, and figured she'd hand the burden over to me, then all would be well.

Polly will take care of it. How many times had I heard that in my life?

I was glad God had given Conrad the grace to be with Rene. She needed his stability right now, not mine. I sat back on the bed, searching for an excuse to give Rene so I could start my investigation. It surprised me that they'd questioned Spencer before Mom, but I didn't doubt that her time would come.

Today I had to start sleuthing, though I knew nothing about it. I'd never even read a mystery. But I did know about photography.

"Actually, I thought I'd take snapshots of the lodge, take advantage of this opportunity. I'll pray for Spencer, though. You should, too."

"What? You think it's so serious that he needs prayer?"

It was serious enough for you to cry. I stifled my exasperation. "One can never pray enough."

"Well, at least you'll be occupied. Conrad and I need some time alone. There's plenty to do here. Hiking and more hiking." She snorted then sounded like she turned her face from the phone. "What else did you say we could do?"

Conrad's muffled answer wasn't clear to me.

"Conrad's not going to wait for Spencer?" I asked.

"He isn't worried. He thinks it's much ado about nothing. But I'm concerned."

"I'm sure he's right." I wished I could be as sure as I sounded. But I knew that Conrad was merely hoping to focus Rene's attention on other important matters—like their upcoming nuptials. We said our good-byes.

I breathed in deeply, grateful for the time alone with my thoughts. Except something niggled at the edge of them. What was I forgetting?

Mom. Of course. How could I have forgotten? I started to phone her then noticed the blinking light that indicated a message. They'd installed voice mail at the historical lodge. Impressive. Mom had left a message while I was on the phone, stating she planned to have breakfast downstairs then do some exploring. Still fighting a headache, she expected to take a nap later.

I didn't have the chance to see Mom too often. Rene's wedding at Caldera Lake had a dual purpose for me. Hence, I was torn between sleuthing and spending time with Mom. I showered and dressed, all the while praying for Spencer. But the more I prayed, the more troubled I became.

Memories of my whirlwind relationship with Spencer played before my eyes like a movie reel. I'd witnessed him lose his temper before. He'd been protective of his younger sister, coming unglued when a boyfriend had dropped her off in tears and with a bruise. I'd peered out the window, watching the confrontation in horror, afraid Spencer would kill Elisa's boyfriend with the punches he threw. It was a side to him I would never have guessed. Still, it was hard to stand in judgment, because the jerk had physically hurt his sister. Spencer took his role as protector seriously.

Fortunately an onlooker had intervened and saved the boy-friend from Spencer's wrath. I'd never seen him lose his temper like that and hoped it was a rare thing. I had to consider that under the right circumstances, he could indeed kill someone.

I finished making up the bed, a chore I never left for the maids. After plumping up a pillow, I slumped against it. Was there more to Spencer's confrontation with Alec? Had he followed him to the hotel room? Had they'd shared more words—heated words that exploded into something physical? People were often slain under such circumstances. Though I felt it completely out of character for Spencer, the day his rage appeared on behalf of his sister had also been a surprise to me. I hadn't seen him in years until yesterday.

Had he mellowed over time like an eighties rock star, or had his inner rage grown?

A chill crawled over me. I grabbed my jean jacket.

In the bathroom, I took a last look in the mirror to fix my hair before leaving. I'd been praying all morning, and as I stared at the mirror, my own guilt stared back. All this time I'd spent as judge and jury for Spencer, bringing his past into it. What about my own?

I rushed to grab my camera, not wanting to face the truth right now. This wasn't about me. It was about Spencer and Mom. Fear gripped me. How deep would the rangers dig? Would they discover my grudge against Alec? Resentment was never something to carry around, but I now saw that mine had festered into bitterness. If I wished Alec dead at one time, did I really mean it? Did God count the thoughts from my heart as actions?

A last glance at my tidied room and I left. But exiting the room didn't help me escape my guilt. God said He would never leave me, and true to His word, He tagged along with me right out the door. I prayed for forgiveness, needing help with my bitterness. I'd never really wanted Alec dead, had I? In fact, I had prayed that he would come to know the Truth. Still, heat rushed over my face. I feared I would look guilty to the ranger who questioned me. Could he detain me for a guilty heart? And if I confessed my grudge toward Alec, would they believe my innocence?

The elevator delivered me to the lobby. I rushed through the lobby and out into the open, fresh air. Even though it was seventy degrees and July, there was a chill in the breeze. I tugged my jacket closed and zipped it. Time to get serious. I had work to do. If everything went as planned—*Lord, please direct my path*—then I would have photos of the historic lodge, and I would run into someone who knew Alec Gordon. Someone other than Mom, Spencer, and myself.

The stone sidewalk led me away from the lodge. I turned to face the building, capturing the images on my camera. So much had happened inside those walls. I allowed my imagination to carry me away as I took more snapshots—always sure to frame things with the rule of thirds in mind. A tree that looked to be decades old, if not centuries, stood firmly planted at the far right corner of the lodge. Yellow and purple pansies encircled its trunk—the entire scene a beautiful accent. I stepped back a smidgen, but something solid blocked my backward momentum.

"What the—," a gravelly voice cried out.

I lost my footing and toppled over the object onto my bottom, my only concern my camera, which I protected from the impact. If there was an advantage to extra pounds in the seat, I'd just discovered it. Sprawled on the lawn, I made sure that my camera was unharmed.

A man took his time crawling out from under my legs and stood. After he'd finished groaning, he extended his hand to me. "You all right?"

Holding my camera, I attempted to stand without his help. I didn't feel confident taking his hand after watching him struggle to his feet. But he grabbed me and set me right. I probably looked like I'd been playing in my mother's makeup—huge red cheeks.

I dusted my pants off. "I'm so sorry. I don't know what happened."

"Nothing to be sorry for. Was my fault." He stooped to recover a trowel.

In addition to the gardening tools, I noticed the brown and green stains on his knees. "You're the gardener then?" He must have been digging in the dirt when I backed right over him.

"Groundskeeper, actually. Name's George Hamilton." He extended his dirty hand to shake mine. I could hardly reject it.

"Like the actor George Hamilton?"

He chuckled. "The name anyway."

If George the groundskeeper had access to multiple plastic surgeries to remove what thirty years spent outdoors had done, then I could see some resemblance. "Pleased to meet you, George."

He picked up his gloves. "I like to feel the dirt with my bare hands." When he turned his palms over, I noticed a cut.

"You're bleeding." I hoped I hadn't caused it.

"No problem. My wife works wonders with her natural remedies. She'll have me fixed up in no time."

He tilted his head toward my camera. "So you're a photographer?"

I nodded. Not too many tourists carried around a Nikon of professional quality, though some serious hobbyist might. George noticed the difference. His observation got me to thinking. "Say, since you know the grounds, how about a behind-the-scenes tour? I'm hoping to do an article to go with my photos."

A distant, thoughtful look in his eyes, George wiped his brow with a rag then scratched his head with his still-dirty hand. "Can't say I've ever done that before."

Now it was my turn to scratch my head. I ran a mental list of excuses I could use to convince him, if needed.

"When did you want to do this?" He glanced down at his work clothes.

"I don't want to inconvenience you or get you in trouble. But now is as good a time as any." I held my breath. A tour of the grounds, including places that others might never see, was exactly the thing I needed to jump-start my amateur investigation of Alec Gordon's death.

"As long as you don't mind my appearance." He jammed his rag in his back pocket so that half of it hung out like a small tail. "Let me put my tools away." He pointed out a building across the parking lot in a wooded area.

"I'll follow you."

His long legs made bigger strides than my short ones, and I had to work to keep up as we crossed the parking lot. A ranger driving a park services vehicle stopped to let us pass then continued on and parked in a reserved spot in front of the lodge. I tried not to worry about Spencer, because I needed to focus on gathering information from George—information that could possibly help Spencer or Mom, if needed.

We arrived at the building that blended into the wooded area. George unlocked the door and went inside to store his implements. I didn't go with him but focused my camera on the lodge. I zoomed in for a closer look at several park services cars and a few state police cruisers. Another chilly breeze gusted, whipping my hair across the lens. I wondered if George would offer his thoughts or if I would have to coax information from him. My palms began to sweat.

Once the door was secured, he turned his attention to me. "What would you like to see first?"

"Just walk and tell me about things as you see them."

For the next hour, George showed me everything from the

flower-trimmed grass surrounding the lodge and parking lot to picnic areas positioned within various groves of trees distanced from the lodge. He'd even begun a project to complement a newly added atrium with local plants inside the east side of the lodge.

George captivated me with his tour of the grounds. He was warm and friendly but never mentioned a word about the murder or Alec Gordon. I could feel the disappointment surface, though I tried to hide it.

After showing me the atrium, he led me outside once more, where we walked along the lake rim until we were far enough away that I could photograph the lodge, which enfolded the rim. From here, I could see the Terrace Café as well.

"And this is about the extent of the grounds that I oversee. Except I do help the tour guides, if someone's sick. They let me keep my boat at the lodge dock, too."

My spirits lifted as I gazed through the lens at a wide angle. "Yes, this is a beautiful place to get married."

"Married, you say? Are you planning your wedding here?"

His question stunned me for a moment because I hadn't realized I'd spoken my thoughts out loud. That habit kept getting worse, which scared me. I was destined to become my mother, with her enlarged space bubble. "Oh, no, I'm not. I'm here to attend a friend's wedding."

"Is that right?" He inclined his head and nodded.

"It must be wonderful to work here, to see this beauty on a daily basis. I admit I'm a tad jealous."

He laughed, giving the half grin that I'd grown to like. "No need to be jealous. Every job has its problems. Even mine."

His comment was the first thing he'd said that gave me an

opening. "Come on George, what problems could you have?"

"I hope your friends have the stick-to-it thinking to make a marriage last. I work hard on mine, but there's still always that worry."

He'd not exactly answered my question about his job, but I was still intrigued. I tried to take pictures that included him as he talked. His face exuded character, and I caught a perfectly framed snapshot of him, looking rugged, with the lodge behind him in the distance. Look out, George Hamilton the actor.

"What worry?" I hoped he would keep talking.

The conversation had turned personal for some reason. Obviously George's marriage had been on his mind lately. My comment about the wedding was all it had taken to bring it out. Too bad he hadn't been thinking about Alec Gordon.

"That she'll leave me."

"Surely not."

"I've been through a lot. The truth is, if I don't keep this job, I might lose her again."

Ah. So his job problem was intertwined with marital discord. Not so unusual. I felt I was intruding by taking photos, but I was afraid that lowering my camera might distract him, stop him from talking.

"You seem like you're doing a fine job here. I can't imagine why you'd fear losing it."

Deep lines edged his frown. "I'm not sure it matters how good of a job I do anymore. But I'm not going to stand for someone threatening me."

His words held a warning in them. I lowered my camera to stare, his stern expression surprising me. Though I was curious about who had threatened his job and why, the sense stirred inside that I had to steer the conversation now or lose it altogether. I hadn't exactly lived up to Spencer's claim that I always got to the point. My conversation with George had strayed under my ill-equipped shepherding, but I would remedy the problem now.

If Alec frequented the park as he said, then George might know something. "What do you think about the murder?"

A cold, sharply angled stone slab, like those he'd used to besiege his flower beds, replaced the warm and friendly George. He drew his gaze from the lake and looked through me, not at me. "Nothing is ever what it seems on the surface, Miss Perkins. You remember that. Good day to you." With that, he left me standing there.

I watched him walk away, feeling like I'd bungled everything. Once he was out of sight, I headed down the sidewalk toward the lodge. A tall, familiar figure in the distance waved.

Spencer?

Relief blew through me as I rushed downhill. Before I realized it, I was in his arms. The joy at seeing him washed all the tension away. When he loosened his grip, I came to my senses and stepped away.

He smiled. "You missed me."

His statement caught me off guard. Rather than consider the matter, I changed the subject. "They let you go?"

His eyes grew wide, then he laughed. "But of course. You act as though I'm guilty."

"That's not what I meant." Tension rushed back into my neck. I looked away.

"You're upset. What's going on?"

"I've spent the last hour or so with the groundskeeper, hoping to gather information about the murder. But I think I botched it."

A strange, incredulous laugh escaped him. "Are you telling me that you're sleuthing? As in. . ." He snapped his fingers, ticking off milliseconds while he tried to remember a name. That was the first time I'd seen him without the right word.

With pleasure, I beat him to it. "Jessica Fletcher in *Murder, She Wrote*."

The right corner of his mouth lifted, revealing his dimple. "But Polly, you can't be serious?"

I suppose he thought his smile would soften the question, but his words burned me, and I hoped he felt the venom I intended. "Yes, I am serious. I don't believe I can leave the lives of those I care about in someone else's hands."

"Not even God's?" Spencer sobered.

"I'm asking Him for help."

He rubbed his hand over his chin, looking more haggard than I'd ever seen him. "Well, I'm going to help, too. Tell me everything. I want in on every detail."

His words were forceful, controlling even. My earlier thoughts regarding his temper raced through my mind. Why? Why did he need to be "in on every detail"?

Judging by the circles under his eyes, his experience with the rangers must have been difficult. Especially if he had something to hide.

Oh, Spencer. I hope you didn't follow Alec to that room.

CHAPTER ⛩ SEVEN

If only I'd read a few Nancy Drew mysteries as a girl, then I'd be prepared to follow the clues left by the killer or at the very least find them. But I hadn't. My mind muddled with confusing thoughts about the whole incident, I needed a fresh perspective. Clean air to clear my head and new scenery for my camera would solve my immediate problem.

Hence, I stood in line behind ten people to sign up for the boat tour of the lake. It was already nine in the morning, and the next tour wouldn't start until eleven. At the speed I gathered information on Alec's murder, the rangers would have Mom put in prison before I had my first solid clue, and if not Mom then probably Spencer. The feeling that the rangers would find one of them guilty wouldn't leave me.

Spencer had looked frazzled after his questioning, which didn't help me shake the notion he was hiding something. Though he insisted he join my amateur investigation, he recommended we work on our own to cover more ground. This surprised me, but I resolved to believe he needed time to collect his thoughts, as would I once the rangers took me aside to grill me. I hoped

Spencer would fare better at sleuthing than I had. With a little help from above, we might know something by this afternoon. I thought more about my conversation with George. He'd not given me much, but perhaps I shouldn't give up on him yet. All I could do from this point was learn from my mistakes. Next time I had the opportunity to talk to someone about the murder, I planned to be forthright. Spencer had commented that I was always to the point, but that wasn't the case when it came to investigating murder. Still, the first step in making progress was to recognize one's weakness.

My turn at the boat-tour desk finally came. I signed my name for the appropriate time slot. I'd purposefully hidden my wallet deep in my bag so I'd have to search for it, giving me time for a short conversation, which I hoped would provide me with clues, glorious clues.

I took a breath as I continued to dig. "So, what do you think about all this hullabaloo?"

"Hullabaloo?" The young blond girl behind the counter smiled.

I wanted to slap my forehead, but I kept a straight face. Why had that word popped into my head? A short time around Spencer, and I'd slipped into using one of his father's words? "Well, um, yes. You know. . .all this hubbub about the murder?" I handed over my credit card.

"Well, I'm not sure what 'hubbub' is either, but I gather you either mean what do I think about the murder, or what do I think about the commotion it's causing?"

Suddenly feeling old, I sighed. "Whichever." I couldn't even ask a simple question.

"Honestly, I try not to think about it too much; that way it won't affect me." She handed the card back. I signed for the charge and tried to hide my astonishment at her attitude.

Disappointed, I nodded then grimly left the counter to go back to my room where I could decompress until the tour. Time locked on a boat with a few passengers would hopefully produce good results. In the meantime, I had to devise a methodology to interrogating—was there such a thing?

On the trek back to the lodge, I worked to create specific, easy-to-understand questions. Once in my room, I wanted nothing more than to take a long, hot bath. Delving into a murder mystery made me feel dirty, but it had to be done—Mom was in deep.

I hadn't seen her this morning, and I needed to check on her. If she was napping, I didn't want to wake her. Still, if she'd taken one of her sleeping pills, a phone call might not disturb her.

I needed to hear her voice, so I opted to at least try. She sounded horrible. Instead of napping, she'd been suffering with a stomach ailment. I didn't doubt the source of her illness lay with her announcement that she'd wanted to kill someone who'd ended up dead mere hours later. I told her to call me if she needed anything then hung up.

Briefly I wondered what Rene and Conrad were doing. What trails they'd decided to hike. I hadn't spoken with Rene since our conversation earlier that morning, nor had I seen them roaming the grounds. Time spent together should solidify their upcoming nuptials all the more, so I put aside any concerns I had about them.

While I filled the tub with hot water, I tried to relax and pray. But too much had happened in a short period of time, and my mind couldn't let go of the many thoughts clamoring for attention.

This weekend was ranking high on my worst-time-ever list, which included the weekend my husband, Brandon, disappeared. Before that, my worst weekend had included Spencer. I'd been much younger then and considered our split to be the breakup of the century. Looking back now, I saw that I'd made a terrible mistake in my attempt to force his hand. Without a commitment from him, I believed I needed to move on. It had taken Brandon walking into my life to patch up my wounded heart.

But I never loved him. Not like I'd loved Spencer.

I slid under the water and wet my hair. I had to bury this line of thinking.

After soaking for twenty minutes, I stepped from the tub. In the mirror, I examined the newest wrinkles around my eyes. It had been ten years since I first met Spencer. Now that he was back in my life—in a manner of speaking—his entrance was no less grand than his exit.

A knock at the door caused a mad dash from the bathroom. I looked from my old sweats on the bed to the clothes hanging in the closet. My hair was a wet, tangled mess. The knock became insistent. I relaxed. Spencer would have spoken through the door by now.

"Just a minute." I pulled on the T-shirt and sweats I usually slept in. Then it occurred to me that it could be a ranger. What if my number had come up—they'd discovered my connection to Alec? I drew in a quick breath then opened the door.

A woman with black hair stood in my doorway. Was she the same woman from the restroom last night? Her black hair was styled the same, but her appearance was somehow different. "Emily?"

"Excuse me?" Her eyes widened.

Then I knew it was her. "Did I say that out loud?"

The smallest of smiles crept over her lips, then she hardened her expression. "I need to talk to you. May I come in?"

Considering there was a killer out there somewhere, I wasn't sure letting her in would be wise. I studied her as I pondered the question. Now I saw what was different from the night before. She brandished two nose piercings, one upper-lip piercing, and a small tattoo on her bare shoulder, none of which matched the emerald-cut diamonds in her ears. She'd gone with a considerably darker look today than last night. Whereas before, she could almost have been called cute in her gothic dress, today she was downright scary. But I should be accustomed to that sort of fashion abuse by now. Such atrocities abound these days.

"I'm not sure that's such a good idea. What's this about?"

"Look, I'm not a murderer, if that's what you're thinking."

I'd never been face-to-face with a murderer, and at that moment, I was sure I wouldn't know if I had, but she brandished no weapon. "All right. You'll have to excuse my appearance though."

She stepped into the room and looked around, her gaze stopping to rest on my camera, which sat next to my laptop. This would be a perfect time to work on my questioning technique— that is, after I found out why she'd come.

"So what did you need to speak to me about?" Had she dropped something in the restroom and thought I'd found it?

"You have to destroy any pictures you've taken that include me."

Now it was my turn. "Excuse me?"

"You don't have any right to take pictures of me."

I closed my eyes, both stunned at her demand and mentally

flicking through the snapshots I'd taken over the last two days. I'd been steeped in a portrait studio for so many years, I wasn't certain that there weren't laws on the matter.

Before I could respond, she continued. "Look, in case you work for a newspaper or magazine or even something on the Internet, I'm warning you. . . ." Then she glared at me.

At that instant I remembered that I'd seen her before we met in the restroom. She was the woman who had practically glared through my camera lens at me yesterday by the lake rim. I resisted the urge to shudder. How had she known where my room was? Had she followed me?

I combed my fingers through my hair and stared back. Was she hiding from someone or running from the law? Shouldn't she have simply avoided me, rather than arouse my curiosity? I wanted to ask more about her warning but thought better of it. I was more concerned about finding Alec's killer.

"All right." I moved away from her and over to my camera then glanced back.

Her eyes widened, giving me the impression she'd been expecting an argument. She nodded and put her hand on the doorknob, preparing to leave.

But I couldn't let her do that yet. I ran my fingertips over my camera. "Did you know Alec Gordon?" Even if they hadn't released the name of the murder victim, I felt sure the news would have spread all over the lodge by now. Unofficially.

The woman stared at me, as if caught off guard yet again. "I've never met him, no."

The way she said "him" conveyed emotion. My breath came quicker. I'd looked at hundreds, even thousands of people's eyes over the years as I'd taken their portraits. I'd developed an instinctive ability to read hidden expressions. But could I use this gift for sleuthing? Emily had proven that I'd been right when I felt her glare was warning me not to take her picture.

But that gift usually showed up when I examined the photographs themselves. I wasn't sure I could read Emily by the way she'd spoken a word.

I had to keep her talking, see if she would reveal anything. "He was a regular guest here at the lodge, you know. Do you come here often, too?"

Her brows wrinkled when she attempted her you-must-be-crazy look, the same one as the night before, except today I saw obvious fear in her eyes. "That's none of your business." She slipped through the door, looking like a gangly teenager with her awkward gait. It was as if she weren't accustomed to wearing those shoes.

Strange, very strange. I decided I'd keep the name—Emily the Strange—I'd given her.

I plopped onto the bed, breathless. There was no doubt I'd read fear in the young woman's eyes. Was she afraid I'd publish a photograph of her? Or had my question about Alec sparked the fear?

I wondered if the two things were related—something like the old saying: Which came first, the chicken or the egg?

Things were strange indeed, Emily.

She was obviously more worried about her photograph appearing somewhere than she was about broaching the topic with me, alerting me she had troubles. But panic hadn't flashed through her eyes until I'd questioned her about Alec Gordon.

She hadn't answered me, but I saw the lie all the same—she had a connection to Alec Gordon. Just how big or small I wasn't sure, but I had to find out.

Now was the time to look through my photographs. I sat at the small desk, wondering if I would actually delete photographs of her if I found any. I loaded the files from my camera onto my laptop and began browsing through the images. Many of the nature scenes pleased me, but I kept my focus on searching for Emily. I couldn't remember if I'd actually pressed the button that would capture her picture when I'd seen her yesterday, or if she'd given me her warning look in time. Scanning through the pictures, I was careful to avoid the ones of Alec's body because I wasn't prepared to face those yet.

One picture caught my attention. I zoomed in on a photo I'd taken of a copse of trees in the distance. With so many people milling about, it wasn't easy to capture nature unhindered. Often, I'd crop the shot if people were in the way. In this particular shot, I'd caught George. I hadn't met him yet when I'd taken it. He was talking to none other than Alec Gordon. I leaned back in the chair, considering what that meant.

George knew Alec.

I moved to the next image. Alec had turned his back to George and faced the camera. I zoomed in on George's expression and gasped. He looked like a man who wanted to kill Alec right there and then.

CHAPTER EIGHT

They'd suggested it would take a full hour to get to the dock, which, at the time, had seemed odd to me. The distance from the lodge to the other side of the lake, where the Feldman's Shore trailhead began, was seven miles. It would only take a few minutes for me to drive there. The trail itself was not even a mile. Now, as I stared at the trailhead that would take me to the lake, comprehension dawned—with a seven–hundred–foot drop to the trailhead, I wouldn't hike this in record time.

Footsteps approached from behind, alerting me that I stood in the middle of the trail entrance. I stepped back rather than down. A guy stood next to me and gazed at the zigzagging trail— or at least what could be seen from our perch. I didn't have long to wait for his reaction.

"Ooohh. So that's why." He said it more as a matter of fact than with a sense of dread.

As he bounded down the trail, he looked like a whippersnapper to me, making me feel old. As they say, you're as young as you feel. At that point, I hoped my body was in better shape than my mind. I picked my way downward as people passed me both going down and coming up. Embarrassed that I was the slowest hiker, I tried to speed up but made a new discovery. My knees were not prepared for this type of descent—forty-five minutes of it— and they screamed in defiance. I was glad I'd made this excursion without Rene, who was in great shape, even approaching forty. If she saw me like this, she'd never leave me alone, calling me at the crack of dawn to make sure I did morning calisthenics.

Finally I stepped onto the dock area where the tour boat awaited. Gulping for air, I leaned against the railing until I recovered. Did they provide a helicopter lift at the end of the day for people who couldn't make their way back? The way I felt at the moment, I hoped so. The last person in line climbed into the boat—my cue to do the same.

A gusty breeze caught my hair, whipping it this way and that, as the tour boat sliced through the pristine lake. I tilted my head back to allow full sun exposure. At such a moment, I didn't care about the dermatologists' warnings against too much sun—more vitamin D was in order. In fact, I'd say a tour of the lake was just what my therapist would have prescribed—that is, if I had one.

Though I'd believed I'd done nothing but bungle my amateur investigation so far, I began to see that I had clues. Nothing concrete yet, but George knew something about Alec, and Emily had stated she didn't know him, although I thought she'd lied. But so what? Even if I managed to question all the guests at the lodge and every tourist at the park and discovered each person gave an answer or reaction that could be construed as they knew something about Alec, would it help my personal investigation? I had nothing by which to measure such vague leads.

Then I remembered the blond at the ticket counter—there was at least one person who knew zilch and didn't seem to care that someone had been murdered. My initial reason for the tour was to organize my thoughts and take photographs. But here I sat on a boat with a captive audience, in a manner of speaking. I knew I couldn't let the opportunity pass.

Surrounding me were people of all ages, wearing jackets or hooded Windbreakers of various shades of blues, reds, and greens, plus a few in the popular camouflage pattern. The tour boat seemed more like a small barge, lined with enough benches to seat twenty.

From his seat in the back of the boat, the tour guide introduced himself as simply Peter. He addressed us over a speaker, droning on about Caldera National Park and explaining the formation of the caldera, or bowl, when the land collapsed after the volcano's eruption. In photographer's heaven, I took plenty of snapshots. The color of the lake had always fascinated me—I'd never seen anything in nature that matched the striking blue.

The tour guide promised we would have ample opportunity to ask questions once he'd finished his monologue. I planned to hold him to that. He'd not been specific about topics, though he probably hadn't meant questions about the murder.

As I gazed through the lens into the depths of the lake, I imagined what it would feel like to dive under the surface with an underwater camera. The thrill of the idea almost washed away the image of Alec's lifeless face, which had never left me. I wondered if it ever would. Thoughts of Spencer vied for attention as well. But the images brought back to mind my objective—to gather clues and find the killer.

With each new conquest, I improved my sleuthing abilities, feeling most confident when reading emotions from behind the camera lens.

The tour guide paused. When the man who'd been hogging his attention had left his side, I gave up my spot on the boat and moseyed next to him, taking snapshots of the rim of the bowl that edged the lake. Even from inside the caldera, lofty peaks could be seen in the distance; some still boasted snow.

When Peter noticed me, I lowered my camera. "It's just breathtaking. You must enjoy giving these tours."

He adjusted his cap, his eyes hidden behind dark sunglasses. "It's a living."

Though I thought he'd been a friendly enough guide, upon closer inspection, I decided he was a somber man. I could see him in thirty years as the grizzled old fisherman, Quint, played by Robert Shaw in the movie *Jaws*, telling tales of a great white beast rather than quoting facts about the lake-filled caldera.

But unlike Quint, who I imagined would smell like rotting fish, this man smelled of cloves. Because I'd blundered by delaying in questioning George, I didn't want to waste time with Peter. Emily's words came back to me: *You don't have any right to take pictures of me.*

"Do you mind if I take your picture? You know how we tourists are."

He shrugged.

After focusing my lens, I asked, "So what do you think about the murder?"

Even with high-speed continuous shooting and several frames per second, I knew that Peter's expression would be difficult to determine because his sunglasses masked his eyes. Much about reading emotions could only be found there.

He didn't answer at first, leaving me to believe he would carefully choose his words. "A helicopter crashed into the lake years ago." He'd slipped back into my impression of Quint and his fisherman's tales.

"That's terrible. Were there any survivors?" I lowered my camera again, noting that Peter had avoided my question.

"No survivors."

I wondered at the pristine lake, promoted as being one of the purest. "Were they able to remove the helicopter?"

"No."

How could I broach a subject that he evidently wasn't willing to discuss? It was as if he'd memorized his spiel about the lake and managed to answer questions but couldn't be expected to make conversation. Well, at least, conversation about murder.

"You asked about the murder," he said.

I cocked my head and nodded. Obviously I'd dismissed him too soon.

"It would have been better to die in that helicopter than to be stuffed in the bottom of a closet. That's what I think."

Aghast at his words, I wasn't sure how to proceed. "I. . .um, I suppose so. But the crash was an accident, not a murder."

"Maybe. Makes you wonder why someone didn't push Gordon off the rim into the lake instead. A two–thousand–foot fall is a sure death and much easier to call an accident."

I'd asked for it, now what was I supposed to do? Maybe I should come right out and ask the man if he killed Alec Gordon.

"You're not a reporter, are you?" He tilted his head.

"Oh, no. I own a family portrait business on the coast. I'm just here for a wedding and thought I'd take a few snapshots. Caldera Lake is so beautiful—" I almost bit my tongue as I tried to stop the flow of words, sounding entirely too eager to tell him what I was doing in an effort to hide what I was doing. I held my breath, hoping he'd believe I wasn't a reporter, although I *was* snooping.

He nodded and pulled off his sunglasses to squeeze the bridge of his nose. A faraway look appeared in his eyes. "My brother-in-law was flying the chopper at the time of the crash. He was a scoundrel. Deserved to die. Any man who'd cheat on his wife or with someone who's married deserves no better." His knuckles turned white as he squeezed the railing.

My throat grew tight, making it hard to swallow. This was big. Really big. I lifted my camera and looked to a lofty peak in the distance. "So, do you think Alec Gordon deserved to die?" I zoomed in and turned the lens on Peter before he could refuse me. Even if he did, I could hopefully read his eyes.

He turned away just as I took the shot. The back of his head was completely devoid of emotion. Big surprise. He'd been forthright, opened up to me. Maybe if I shared more about myself, he would as well—sort of a give-and-take relationship.

I opened my mouth to say something, but another woman's words filled the gap. She'd gained Peter's attention from his other side. After a few minutes it became apparent that I'd lost my opportunity. Not only had Peter avoided answering my question, he'd not given me the chance to capture his expression.

Had he known that his expression would give him away?

I took the empty seat on a bench next to an Asian couple who were busy taking pictures. As soon as they saw my camera, they jabbered on about it, though I couldn't understand a word they said. No point questioning them.

The boat docked next to Thomason Island—a small volcanic cinder cone that formed an island at the north side of the lake. Peter explained that anyone who chose to hike the island would have to wait until the evening to be picked up. Two young men hopped out of the boat; one I recognized from the top of the trail.

I moved to the railing as others gathered to look at the island.

A silver-haired woman next to me spoke in hushed tones to her husband. "If only the beauty weren't shadowed by this murder."

Once we headed away from the island and people repositioned themselves, I made sure I sat next to the couple. All I could glean from them was they'd been briefly interviewed and were free to leave but wanted to tour the lake. They planned to cut short their stay at the lodge because of the murder.

I approached a woman with a young boy whom I assumed was her son. Before I could open my mouth, she quickly scooted her son away from me, unsettling me. Had I been too obvious in questioning people about the murder? I glanced about for other prospects, but the boat was already nearing the dock.

The tour ended too soon. A man assisted the tourists off the boat. I was last in line, and when it was my turn for help, Peter took the man's place and gripped my hand to pull me up onto the dock.

He removed his sunglasses and cap. "How would you like a private tour of the island? I'd be happy to assist, if you're interested."

Because of his comments about a better way to have murdered Alec, his offer alarmed me. "Um. . ."

"Since you're a photographer, I thought you'd like to see more than the average tourist." He shoved his hat back on and put his sunglasses in place, ending my scrutiny.

He smiled, disarming me. It transformed him from Robert Shaw in *Jaws* to a suave, young Ewan McGregor in *Big Fish*. Still, it was hard to dispense with the grizzly character I'd painted on him like the name on a boat.

Part of me felt like he toyed with me, but the other part told me I was a paranoid fool. I returned his smile with a cautious grin. "That sounds like fun."

I'd have to think long and hard about it, but I probably wouldn't see him again anyway.

I started the arduous climb up the steep trail and back to the lodge, somehow feeling like I'd betrayed Spencer, because I'd been gone for so long and because another man had asked me to go somewhere with him.

Concern over his possible role in Alec's demise was slowly fading. In fact, now that I considered it, my fears about Spencer were muted against the backdrop of George's murderous glare and Peter's strange words. No way was Spencer a cold-blooded killer. But doubt still niggled at me. What if it was an accident? I wanted to hear from Spencer that he'd not followed Alec. But on this, there was no getting to the point. I hoped it would somehow come out without me asking. Otherwise, I'd be admitting I could think such a thing of him. In his eyes, that would be unforgivable.

I'd just shut the door behind me in my room when the phone rang.

"Hello?"

"Polly, it's Spencer." He sounded upset.

I imagined that he'd seen me agreeing to a date with Peter, though he couldn't have. "Spencer, what is it?"

"The authorities have taken your mum for questioning. She was in hysterics. I've been looking for you everywhere."

"Oh no!" Guilt and worry flooded me. I was taking entirely too long to find someone else with motivation to kill Alec.

"Polly. Why didn't you tell me of your mum's business deal with Alec?"

CHAPTER NINE

I paced across the claustrophobic space of my room, wishing I had at least one of Mom's nervous habits with which to expend energy. "I don't know why I didn't tell you."

I wondered if someone had reported hearing her outburst at the Terrace Café—something else I'd kept from Spencer. I supposed I'd hoped that by keeping quiet, it would simply go away.

"I can't help if you don't tell me everything."

"When did they take her?" I'd known her time would come, but I feared for her nonetheless. "Oh, why did I leave her?"

If she were in hysterics as Spencer had said, then I could see her confessing to the murder whether she'd done it or not. I imagined Mom in a dark, wet dungeon—somewhere I'd never see her again.

"Calm down. I don't need two of you in an uproar. Your mum was enough to handle as it was. She's been gone a couple of hours. I expect if her experience is anything like mine, she'll be back soon."

"I hope you're right."

"Polly, if I'd known about Alec's scam sooner, I could have

looked into it. We might have solved this already."

Why does hindsight always confront us with a trail of wrong decisions? Then it hit me. "How did you find out about the scam?"

"I was with her when the ranger came through the lobby doors. He made a beeline for us."

"But she was sick in her room earlier this morning and wanted to rest. That's why I left her."

"She must have recovered. No, wait, she was looking for you. Now that you mention it, she looked a little pale. But I assumed that was because the ranger came for her. Before he reached us, she told me Alec had scammed her on a real estate deal, but she didn't kill him. Wait a sec. . ." Spencer spoke to someone in a muffled voice then came back. "Sorry, about that—"

"Who's there with you? Are you in your room?"

"No, I'm in the atrium. Have you seen it? It's beautiful."

"You're on your cell? How do you do that?" I'd failed to get a signal even once and had decided the place was a dead zone.

"It's quite simple, actually." Spencer began a spiel about how cell towers work.

"Stop, that's not what I meant. Just get back to Mom's story."

"Right-o. I'm not sure why she wanted to explain it to me. But when they told her they needed to question her, she became a basket case. It worried me because. . .Polly, frankly. . .she acted guilty."

I sighed, distressed with the news. "That's exactly what I was afraid of."

"You don't mean to say she's guilty."

"Of course not! But I was afraid she'd act like she is. That she'd collapse, thinking they'd believe she killed Alec. She has motive and witnesses who heard her say. . ."

"Heard her say what, Polly? What are you talking about?"

"There's something else you might as well know. You aren't the only one who said something stupid at the Terrace Café that people overheard. She said she wanted to kill 'that man.' At the time, of course, I didn't know she meant Alec, and neither did anyone who witnessed it."

Silence lingered as if I'd stunned Spencer with the news. "I can't believe this. Why didn't you tell me?"

"I'm sorry, Spence." So, I'd finally come to the place where I felt comfortable calling him Spence.

Again he was silent, making me crazy. Was he considering what I'd called him—did he like me calling him Spence? Or was he thinking about Mom's outburst?

Never good at staring or quiet games, I caved. "I need to know what you think."

"I think I don't like talking about this over the phone. And Polly, I'd like to know who told the rangers about my row with Alec. Perhaps they did the same with your mum, and maybe they're trying to direct the rangers' attention elsewhere."

"Good point. You might have a clue there. But Mom's experience will be different than yours. She had a reason to want to kill him." As I said the last sentence, I wondered about Spencer's warning to Alec.

"The good news there is your mum probably wasn't the only one with animosity toward Alec Gordon. I've been researching while I waited for you to show up. Decided to take a walk and give you another ring. Glad I caught you."

I slapped my forehead. At this rate, I'd need to purchase some sort of padded headband. With so many things happening, I hadn't had time to look into Mom's business deal. But that would have been the most logical first step in investigating Alec's murder. "Spencer, you're brilliant. You've got a lot to go on already. Maybe between the two of us we can solve this."

"I agree. What do you say we meet?"

"What about the Terrace Café? I haven't had lunch yet."

Propped on the bed, I waited for his answer, which came in the form of a long pause. Immediately I tried to discern what that meant. "Spence, did you hear me?"

"Sorry. Yes, I'll see you at the Terrace Café in say, fifteen minutes?"

"See ya." As soon as I hung up, the phone rang again. It was Mom. "Oh, Polly."

Her next words were unintelligible. Spencer wasn't kidding when he said she was in hysterics. How had the rangers managed to question her at all? "Are you in your room?"

Some semblance of the affirmative answered me.

"I'm on my way."

Still sobbing, she managed to say, "And I only have two sleeping pills left!"

"Mom, I'm hanging up now. I'm coming to your room, okay?" I dragged my words out, hoping she'd grasp them.

I headed out the door and to her room. Mom opened the door before I knocked and let me in. Things were strewn across the floor, over the bed, dresser, and television set. "What happened here?" Had the real killer searched her room while she was gone?

The bed was lopsided under her weight as she slumped on the edge. "I was looking for the extra bottle of pills I brought. I can't find them anywhere." She pressed her hands on her face, but, though I expected her to sob, she remained quiet. Maybe she'd cried all her tears. I hoped so.

As I recalled, she'd stuffed the prescription bottles right back into the sack after she'd showed them to me. No sense in arguing, though. "Everything is going to be fine. You don't need more sleeping pills." *Or cigarettes for that matter.* But I didn't want to mention those, lest she launch into a search for them. "Now, tell me what happened." She proceeded to describe the details of her ride to the ranger station. I chewed on my lip instead of screaming for her to get to the important part.

"And then they questioned me." She began picking up the items she'd tossed about the room as though she had nothing more to say.

Fumes of sulfuric gas had to be coming from my ears. "Mom, I want to know what they asked you. I want to know how you answered."

"Well, why don't you just say so? You asked me what happened. So that's what I told you."

I could see things clearly now. Mom probably knew what she was getting into with Alec regarding his so-called scam. Maybe he hadn't even scammed her. Maybe she wanted to buy a piece of property from him and drove him crazy until he just sold her something that didn't exist. It could happen. . . . As my out-of-control thoughts surged, I rubbed my forehead, recognizing that my survival instincts were kicking in. If it weren't for my strange sense of humor, I'm not sure how I would have survived all these years.

"Okay, so now I'm asking. Please tell me about the interview." At that moment, I needed Rene's lozenges or, God forgive me, Mom's cigarettes! With nothing to diffuse my agitation, I started picking up the clutter, too.

"Polly, I think I have a big mouth." While she folded a shirt, her eyes were riveted on me. "Don't give me that look. I know you've always thought that. Just never said so. Well, at least not in so many words."

Although I'd wanted to have this discussion for years, telling Mom that she let too many people close to her, that her secrets belonged to the entire world because she lacked a volume knob, this wasn't the time. "Please. That has nothing to do with your interview. I want to know, and I want to know now."

"No need to be disrespectful to your mother. I'm getting there. I should never have said those awful words about Alec where others could hear me. I'm not one to care about others' business or to eavesdrop, and I expect the same treatment as well. The ranger—he's very nice, you know—he told me that someone had overheard me say I wanted to kill Alec Gordon."

Actually, she'd not said his name at the time, but I didn't want to cork the flow of words once it started by pointing that out. "Okay, so we know that. Go on."

"I told him why I'd said that. I tried to tell them that I could never kill him, but I was crying so hard I could hardly talk."

If they didn't already have one, I was sure pharmaceutical

companies could make a lot of money on a drug that subdued crying in certain circumstances. "I take it they understood your plea and believed you." *Please, God.*

"He said he might need to ask more questions." She shrugged. "That's it."

"That's it?"

"He asked how long I planned to be at the lodge, and I told him through the weekend."

Relief overwhelmed me, but confusion followed. I turned my back to Mom so she wouldn't see the troubled expression I knew was on my face. Why had they let her go? She'd said she wanted to kill the guy, had the motivation, and now he was dead. This wasn't the end for her, I felt certain. Plastering a smile on my face, I spun to face her again.

She pressed a hand to her cheek. "Rene is still getting married, isn't she?"

I nodded, but gently, so I wouldn't jar the smile I'd weakly glued on. "I think it's for good this time. Did they say what happened to Alec or who they think killed him?" They wouldn't have told Mom, but I hoped she might remember if she'd heard anyone else mention something.

"They told me nothing. Do you think they suspect me?"

I wanted to encourage her, but I didn't know enough about what the rangers were thinking. "It's hard to say. But *you* know that you didn't kill him." If only that were enough.

"But what if they don't? That happens all the time, you know? What if they end up thinking I did it?"

I pressed my lips together and hugged her. I would do

everything in my power to make sure that didn't happen. But I wouldn't tell her about my private investigation yet. "They'll find the real killer, don't worry."

"Until they do, you need to be careful. There was a gardener from the lodge looking for you. I told him I didn't know you. After all, he was a complete stranger. Oh, and I almost forgot. The ranger said he hoped to have someone in custody by the end of the weekend."

I drew in a quick breath.

They would have someone in custody by the end of the weekend? I couldn't believe she'd almost forgotten that small detail. Time wasn't on my side.

But what else had she said? The gardener? How had he known to ask Mom about me? I could only assume that George had seen us together. Had he been watching us?

———

George proved to be ghostlike when it came to finding him. Despite the murderous look he'd given Alec, I liked him and hoped for a suitable explanation. But I reminded myself that meant nothing. Murderers were usually normal, everyday people. If society could tell by looking at a person or talking to them that they had killed someone, we'd have them all locked up today. So although I'd felt a connection with George, I kept the image of his murderous scowl in my mind. I hoped to ask him about it— if I ever found him. It seemed as if Alec was hated enough that if every photograph I'd taken had a shot of him in it, there would be someone scowling behind him.

If looks could kill and so forth. Looks couldn't kill, but passion could.

I cringed as I thought of those who'd had a mad rage against Alec. Mom, Spencer, and George had all three shown a deep and potentially raging anger toward him. Peter had directed his passion elsewhere, but I wondered about a person who could think of a better way to kill someone who'd been murdered, like Peter had.

After searching the grounds George had shown me and asking several passersby if they had seen him, I hiked up a steep trail that looked like it would take me to a high point on the rim. I hoped to take a few snapshots, and possibly, I could see George from there.

Once again, the mesmerizing blue of the lake captivated me. For a moment, I allowed myself to imagine Spencer enjoying the scenery with me.

Spencer.

"Oh no!" I'd forgotten to meet him. What must he think? I worked my camera into the case.

"Heard you were looking for me." George's familiar voice startled me.

The strap around my neck caught my camera when I dropped it. I whirled to face his stern expression. "Well, um. . .yes. Because I heard you were looking for me." I'd hoped to find him on the grounds near the lodge, not alone on the trail. The image of his menacing scowl was still vivid in my mind.

"You shouldn't be out here alone with a killer on the loose."

Could everyone read my mind? The thought almost paralyzed me, considering I'd been thinking of him as the possible murderer.

"Especially with you snooping around, stirring things up." He picked up a stick and beat a patch of dusty earth.

A knot materialized in my throat. I swallowed. "What makes you think that?"

"If I know it, then so does the murderer."

"Well, you're wrong. I'm doing no such thing." Snooping maybe, but not stirring things up.

George tugged his cap and gazed over the lake. "People usually don't pay any mind to me. I guess you could say I'm invisible. That's why I see things without them knowing I'm watching. I've seen you taking pictures and asking about the murder."

A cold wariness gripped me. Did George know that I'd caught him on film scowling at Alec? "It's just curiosity."

"Wanted to warn you. Someone spotted you hiking up here. Folks call you *that photographer*."

The news stunned me. "I can't be the only photographer here. That's absurd."

"No, but you're the only one snooping around. You act like a reporter. Are you?"

"Look, I'm no reporter. I own a portrait studio on the beach, and I'm here for a wedding. I've told you that already." Broaching the subject about his angry scowl now would be tough. This wasn't going at all like I'd hoped.

A couple appeared on the trail, walking toward us.

Since George already considered me a snoop, I forged ahead. "I have a picture of you with Alec. You're standing behind him and look like you could. . .well"—the knot in my throat grew bigger—"kill him. Why were you so angry with him?" I prepared myself for his reaction, thinking I could outrun him, if needed. He was much older, and besides, I felt safe because of the approaching couple. The precarious situation I'd put myself in was almost funny. Almost.

George's expression remained calm, as though he wasn't at all surprised by my question. "What makes you think I'll answer?"

"For one thing, you came up here to warn me." I relaxed a bit. He'd not reacted to my question as if he were a killer—like I knew what that should be.

"Remember when I told you that I wouldn't stand by and let someone threaten to get me fired? Alec threatened me. I can't lose this job, or my wife will leave me this time."

"But why would he do that?"

"Because I saw something I shouldn't have seen, like I always do. But this time, I got caught, like I was spying or something. Guests don't like to think they're being watched, especially by the lodge staff. Believe me, it's best not to pay attention to them or their activities. That can only lead to trouble."

I knew George's words were meant for me. "Go on. I want to know what you saw."

"A couple days ago, a young lady's suitcase flew open, and her stuff flew out all over the place. I was going to help, but Alec got there first. Figured she probably didn't want my dirty hands on her things anyway. I saw Alec pick something up off the ground and stuff it into his pocket. When he looked around to see if anyone had been watching, he noticed me."

"Then he threatened you?"

"That's right. He said he would complain about me, whatever it took to get me fired, if I didn't mind my own business."

"And you believed he could do that?"

"You don't understand." George stared at the ground. "I couldn't risk it. But someone took care of Alec Gordon. So, I don't have to worry about him anymore."

With his straightforward way and his attempt to watch out for me, I could easily think of George as a father figure. My heart warmed at the thought. He reminded me of the father I never had, if I'd never had a father. He just couldn't be the murderer. "Who was the woman he helped, do you remember?"

"She looked like someone from *The Addams Family*. But these days, that's pretty common. You know. . .long, black hair. Everything black. Tattoos. Jewelry in places that weren't meant to have it."

My heart raced. Unless I'd missed someone, Emily was the only person I'd seen this weekend who fit that description. And in that case, Emily had indeed lied to me. Was what Alec had stolen worth his life?

"I like you. That's why I'm going to say again, nothing is ever what it seems. Be careful."

George liked me? So, was he the killer, and he was warning me so he wouldn't have to kill me? My amateur investigation was a tangled web and getting more complicated by the minute. A pounding sensation spread up the back of my head.

I leaned against the railing at the edge of the rim and looked straight down the two–thousand–foot drop.

"It's best if we're not seen walking back together."

"Why not? You don't want anyone to see you talking to the nosy photographer?"

George chuckled, sounding far away.

I turned to see his expression, but he'd vanished from sight. How had he done that? I hiked down the trail, hoping to find Spencer and apologize for the delay in meeting him and to share what George had told me. His warning felt like a two-edged sword, but a gardener would more likely carry a shovel. Though I was glad he'd wanted me to be careful, I sensed there was more to it.

When I approached a well-canopied part of the trail that led back to the lodge, I came to a stop, wishing I'd paid more attention on the way up. For some reason, I couldn't remember these densely knitted trees along the hike. I edged forward into the darkened cathedral-like area, trying to shove aside thoughts of menace and murder, as an irrational fear overtook me. Words I'd brooded over, spoken in connection with Alec's murder, clashed in my head.

I want to kill the man! I told him to stay away from you. . .or else. Makes you wonder why someone didn't push him off the rim into the lake instead. I'm not going to stand for someone threatening me. If I know it, then so does the murderer.

I covered my ears, wanting to drown out the unspoken words. Another sound drew my attention, and I dropped my hands to listen.

A twig snapped from somewhere in the darkened forest, near the trail.

I ran.

CHAPTER ⫼⫼⫼ TEN

The trail ended, and what fear possessed me quickly dissipated upon seeing the busy tourist area. Feeling ridiculous for giving in to an overactive imagination, I stopped to catch my breath and mentally created a sticky note to take up running when I made it home to the beautiful Oregon coast. That is, *if* I made it home. Once my breathing returned to normal, I headed to the Terrace Café. Chances were Spencer had already left, but one could hope. Besides I was thirsty. Thoughts of a nice tall glass of pink lemonade taunted me.

Brightly colored umbrellas came into view as I approached the outdoor restaurant overlooking the lake. In contrast, Emily lounged at one of the tables, sporting gloom and darkness. She was easy to spot—something about that nagged me. My spirits sagged when I didn't see Spencer, but I needed to push forward with the investigation. Considering what George had shared, I intended to pay Emily a visit next.

Though she wouldn't like it, I planned to conduct an interview of sorts through the lens of my camera this time, falling back on one of Mom's favorite sayings: "What she doesn't know won't hurt her." I noticed a perfect table, shaded by a tree rather than an umbrella, at the opposite end of the terrace. The tree would veil my covert observation.

The café was busy with all manner of tourists, lunching and cooling their thirsts amid the smell of grilled chicken and beef. On the far side, I made my way to the table I'd chosen without looking Emily's way, hoping she'd not see me in the crowd. I typically blended in well. That's why what George had said about me earning the nickname "that photographer" struck me as odd.

But I didn't have time to worry about what people thought or said. I prayed I wasn't following the wrong trail. I realized that once I prayed for direction, I could only trust I traveled the right path, unless the dreaded forked road appeared. If I came across that, which way would I choose?

After giving the waiter my order, I gazed through the lens of my camera and pulled out to a wide angle. I then positioned it on the table, giving me the ability to photograph Emily without holding the camera to my face. With the sophisticated photography tools available today, I could zoom in for an even closer look later, using software.

She sat alone, sipping from a disposable cup, which led me to believe she'd purchased her drink to go. Maybe she was waiting for someone. I wished I'd thought to notice at dinner last night who she was sitting with.

A commotion to my left drew my attention. Spencer disentangled himself from a chair he'd fallen over. As he stood, he placed his hand on a table, knocking someone's teacup off.

I cringed at the sight and the awful noise. The only thing worse than a teacup shattering is a fingernail across a chalkboard. I couldn't remember Spencer ever being so clumsy.

He made his way toward me. So much for clandestine sleuthing. Emily couldn't have missed the racket. Certain that she'd spotted me, I willed myself to ignore her glare, pretending I hadn't seen her.

"Polly." Spencer panted like he'd been running. "I've been worried about you. Where've you been?"

"Shh. Sit down and relax. You realize the last time you were here you created a scene, too." With his grand entrance, all eyes were on us. So far, the Terrace Café seemed to act as a studio, producing melodramatic miniscenes.

"Correction. The last time I was here, I was waiting on you."

Ouch. I sucked in air. "Sorry about that." I glanced around to see if anyone was looking. "Let's not draw any more attention to ourselves."

"I agree. How about we discuss something resembling a return to normalcy. That is, after you explain where you've been." He narrowed his eyes.

Such beautiful blue eyes. I didn't miss the sheer relief I saw there, and it pleased me. I smiled in response. "I'm—"

"A delightful sight, that." His eyes softened and crinkled at the corners.

"What are you talking about?"

"Your smile."

I sighed. I couldn't decide if it was in satisfaction or despair. The waiter brought my pink lemonade then took Spencer's order. I'd lost my appetite and wondered about his order of tea but assumed he'd eaten while waiting on me earlier. The reprieve allowed me to collect myself after his obvious flirtation. Maybe later I'd explore what I had to admit was a deep-seated hope of reuniting with Spencer. I was sure wisdom and experience would caution me to let go of that hope.

I glanced in Emily's direction. She'd left her table. "I'm sorry about keeping you, but I was delayed when Mom called."

George warned me against sleuthing. I wondered if sharing the additional information I'd gathered would create concern in Spencer. Would he try to stop me as well?

Spencer gave a courteous nod at the waiter who brought his hot tea with milk. I couldn't imagine how anyone could drink hot tea in the middle of a warm day like this, even at eight thousand feet. But British tradition wasn't to be trifled with.

"How's your mum? What did the police say?"

I tried to remain calm. Getting upset wouldn't help me find the real killer. "Thanks for asking. She's beyond stressed right now. She told them everything about her involvement with Alec and his scam, why she'd said she could kill him."

Spencer looked thoughtful then shook his head. "Say, Polly, after this is over—the investigation and the wedding—I'd love for you to come see my parents' new estate."

My heart rate increased. I didn't want him to see any visible signs of my reaction, such as the pulsing at the hollow of my throat, so I stared at him over the edge of my glass, taking much too long of a drink. Why had he brought this up now?

He leaned closer and spoke in a soft voice. "We were supposed to talk about ordinary things, remember?"

I set my glass down and wiped at the condensation. "Reading my mind again?"

He chuckled. "I suppose I am." His gaze held mine for what seemed like an eternity. If he could read my mind, did he know that I harbored hope for us? Why couldn't I read his in return?

I snatched up my camera, thinking to catch his expression on film so that I could apply my ability to read emotions in photographs to him. Sliding my chair from the table a few inches, I leaned back and focused the lens on the trees behind him, keeping his face in the picture while I took a few snapshots.

"Polly, do you have to do that while we're talking?"

I lowered my camera to look at him. "I didn't realize it bothered you."

"It doesn't, usually. But right now I'd like to have your full attention." His blue-eyed gaze sent a warm sensation through me.

I liked the way he'd said that. "I'm listening."

"My parents bought a historic castle here in the states. Did you know that?"

The news surprised me. "Rene hadn't mentioned anything to me." Come to think of it, Rene hadn't mentioned Spencer in years. "Why did they buy it?"

"It's an old castle. The original owner moved it over, stone by stone."

"Aha. They wouldn't want to purchase anything that wasn't British, would they?" I had long expected that one of the reasons Spencer remained noncommittal to me was his parents. They were British snobs and never liked me, despite that at one time

I'd maintained dual citizenship.

"Now, Polly. Be nice. I thought with your new interest in photographing historic lodges, you'd find it intriguing."

A small laugh escaped me. "My, you're quite observant. I admit I'm a bit charmed by it all." But if I visited Spencer at his parents' estate, I'd risk exposing myself to their ridicule all over again. I'd risk exposing my heart to Spencer, which I couldn't do until I was certain of his intentions. I couldn't allow him to toy with my emotions. Why had he invited me?

I turned to thoughts of historic lodges and took some snapshots of the lodge, focusing on the second floor, the room next to where I stayed in the good old days before the murder.

As I considered whether or not I wanted to visit Spencer's parents' estate, I noticed movement in the window of the room where Alec was murdered. Someone peeked through the curtain. I zoomed in to see if I recognized one of the rangers or detectives, but I couldn't tell.

After taking a few more snapshots, I loaded my camera into the case. Though my mind now spun with thoughts regarding Alec's murder, I hadn't forgotten Spencer's invitation.

Apparently he hadn't either, because he had the expectant look of someone waiting patiently for a response as he studied me.

I inclined my head and peered at him, uncertain how he would take what I had to say. "I'm not sure it would be a good idea."

The lines around his eyes smoothed out as his smile faded. "Why not? Why isn't it a good idea?"

I couldn't bring myself to commit to something I might regret later. Instead of answering, I said, "Come on, Spencer. We've got work to do."

He sighed. I wasn't sure if he was disappointed because we were back to sleuthing or because I hadn't responded favorably to his invitation. Even without my camera I could see a deep sadness and—had I imagined it because I wanted to see it?—longing. Part of me wished I could dispense with all of the misery surrounding matters of the heart and rush into his arms.

But for the moment, one thing stopped me.

Alec Gordon's murder.

———

Spencer joined me in a small, secluded alcove furnished with chairs, a desk, and a small table on the ground floor of the lodge. He thought it would provide enough privacy for us to discuss what we'd discovered thus far about the murder. I'd told him about seeing someone at the window of Alec's room, and we both agreed looking at the snapshots I'd taken was imperative. Though it was only early afternoon, our failed attempts to meet over the last few hours created a greater sense of urgency.

I'd retrieved my laptop from my room and opened it on the desk. "Now that we have some privacy, I'm going to load the photos. Why don't you tell me if you've discovered anything important while we wait."

He pulled up a chair next to me. "Before I forget, I ran into Rene and Conrad while looking for you." He placed strong emphasis on the last three words.

"I hope you didn't tell them anything about our plans to discover who killed Alec Gordon."

He threw his head back and scoffed. "Not a word. They didn't ask, so I didn't tell. They appeared to be in soon-to-be-married heaven."

I wanted to ask him why he'd never married, but that would be a serious detour. I selected the image I wanted to view. "See that? Someone's looking through the curtains."

Spencer shook his head, frowning. "So?"

"Uh, that's the room where Alec was murdered."

"Yes. Well, it's probably someone investigating the crime. They still have the place blocked off. Yellow tape and that sort of thing."

Why had it caught my attention? "Something about the way they're looking through the curtains seems. . .off." I enlarged and enhanced until I could see who it was.

I gasped. "Spencer, it's the woman who discovered the body. The housekeeper."

"I see her." He stood and held his chin. "She couldn't be cleaning, could she?"

"Well there's one way to find out. We can ask her. Or we can go to the room first to see if the yellow tape—whatever they call it—is gone." Had they found the killer? Was the investigation over? How would we know? I moved to close my laptop.

"Wait."

When he didn't continue, I turned my head to look at him.

"Tell me exactly how it happened yesterday. . .when you saw his body."

I'd not told anyone about what I'd experienced. Sure, I'd told the ranger about what I'd seen in the closet, but they'd not questioned me further yet. How much should I tell them? Was my past relationship with Alec relevant? I suppose if they asked me if I knew Alec before, I'd have to tell them we'd gone to school together. Spencer's request brought on a slew of unpleasant thoughts and images. But rehashing those now wouldn't get me anywhere.

"Polly?" He placed his hand on my shoulder. "You all right?"

I swept my hand slowly down my face, but I couldn't wipe the memories from my mind. Spencer sat next to me once again and took my hand—I assumed for a show of support—though I had the strong sense that he wanted to hold me.

After sharing every detail I could remember, I realized it wasn't much at all.

"Polly, you mentioned the horror of it all. But one thing you didn't mention strikes me as odd."

I frowned. "What's that?"

Spencer looked at my camera then back at me. "If I know anything about you, I know that you reflexively take pictures under pressure. It's one of the things I. . ." He trailed off but let his eyes remain on me.

I stared at him, waiting for the rest of the sentence. My better judgment told me not to finish it, but when had I ever listened to my better judgment? Had the rest of the sentence been. . .*love about you?* Suddenly my throat became parched.

Still, just the word "love" didn't offer much hope. Love could be such a generic term in the English language. People love their houses, their cars, their clothes. . . .

"Have you looked at them?" he asked, breaking the spell.

"At what?"

"The pictures—the ones you took of Alec's body."

My mind drew a complete blank at his statement. "No, I. . .

I'm afraid I haven't." I'd not wanted to see them earlier when I'd searched for Emily and found George scowling.

Surprise registered that the ranger hadn't come immediately after me for my photos, if for no other reason. Maybe due to the horror of the event, his subconscious had blocked out the memory that I'd been taking photographs of the body. One could wish. I couldn't remember if he was in the room or not during my snapshot frenzy. It all seemed a blur. Perhaps shock did that to a person.

I scanned through the images, searching. Dread engulfed me. Would seeing Alec's pictures make me relive the moment? "I don't know if I can look."

"Then let me do it."

I moved from the seat, feeling like I was in a daze and wishing I had, in fact, deleted the crime scene pictures. Leaning against the wall next to the desk where I could face Spencer, I watched his expression contort, his frown deepen.

"Oh, Polly. I'm sorry you had to see this." He looked up at me, compassion in his eyes. "I didn't realize how awful it must have been for you." His gaze moved back to the laptop screen.

I studied his eyes, imagining I could see the reflection of the photos there. "I can't take this anymore. I've got to see them, too."

Before he could stop me, I'd rushed around the desk. By the time I could see the screen, he'd managed to bring up the housekeeper's face rather than Alec's body.

"Question. Had she been cleaning the room and discovered the body? Or is there more to it?" he asked.

I studied her face. "I know it sounds crazy. But when I see

faces in photos I've taken, I can read their emotions. Of course, there's no way to know how accurate my methods are."

"And what do you read in her expression?"

"She looks completely distraught."

"And I agree, though I claim no gift." He glanced at me, offering a smile. "Here, you sit now."

I sat at the laptop again, Spencer in the chair next to me.

"But you wonder why she's distraught," I said. "Is it because she killed him or because she found the body?"

"Now you're reading *my* mind."

"Well, there's nothing incriminating here. We have nothing on the housekeeper from these photos until we find out what she was doing in that room today." I positioned the arrow to end the program.

"Wait." Spencer placed his hand on top of mine. "Do you see that?"

The housekeeper gripped something in her hand.

CHAPTER ELEVEN

Even though after enlarging the image and the housekeeper's fist filling the screen, I still couldn't make things out. "What's she holding?"

Spencer squinted. "Looks like a dark red cloth."

"Alec's handkerchief!" We said the words in unison.

"You know about his handkerchief?" I asked.

"Well, I couldn't miss it, not with him blubbering into it. That was his response to my 'or else' warning. It's not likely I'd forget that." Hands in his lap, he looked down, regret twisting his features.

I held my breath. This was the chance I'd hoped for—an opportunity to discover what he'd done after his words with Alec. But how could I ask him?

Before I could think of what to say, he rubbed his eyes and said, "His comments about you made me really angry, Polly. I won't repeat them, but there was a time in my life when I might have done more than give him words. I'd just come out of those troubled college days when you met me."

I touched his hand to reassure him.

A feeble grin crossed his lips, enough to dimple his cheek. "It scares me to think of what might have happened, had I followed him. Not that I would have planned an act of murder."

Relief came in the form of moisture-filled eyes, which I hated. Bring on those prescription drugs to keep the tears at bay. I swiped a hand down my face to disguise wiping them away. "Even if you'd done nothing more than follow him, it would have looked bad for you, given your past temperament."

"Yes. I'm thankful I had an alibi. I ended up talking at length with a guide at the information center by the lake rim to kill time . . .sorry. Poor word choice. I was waiting to see you. As things worked out, I ran into Conrad and Rene when they arrived."

I nodded. "That's why it looked like you'd come with them. Why didn't you find me or call my room if you were so anxious to see me?"

He gave a short laugh. "After all this time, I wasn't sure how you would receive me. I was looking for an approach, the right moment, that sort of thing."

A pensive silence lingered between us. I sensed he wanted to know my reaction, given what he'd revealed. The thought that he'd followed and watched me from a distance didn't sit well with me, but on the other hand, I think I understood why. There was so much I wanted to say—

The screen flickered and drew my attention. "I have to plug this in. The battery is about to go."

Spencer found the wall socket behind the desk as I studied the image on the screen. I needed to bridle the flood of emotions he'd stirred, save the discussion for a more appropriate time.

When he finished connecting the computer, he sat next to me

again. "I'm sorry for laying that on you. Bad timing. We've got a lot of muck to muddle through at the moment." With that, he took my face in his hands and kissed my forehead. "But later. . ."

Spencer had put me in the wrong mood for a murder investigation. It was a struggle to focus on anything but his nearness, despite the pressing circumstances.

I attempted to bring the conversation back to our sleuthing efforts and looked at the monitor. "So, if that's his handkerchief, then why is the housekeeper holding it? I think we might have our first real clue. All I have to do now is show these photos to the ranger, right?"

Spencer placed his hand over his mouth in a thoughtful pose before finally responding. "Hold up, Polly. We haven't got much of anything. She could have found it on the floor while cleaning then opened the closet door."

I felt like a balloon blown up with hope then deflated with reality. "You're right, of course. We need to find out more about her."

"How? With more pictures?" His reproachful tone made me tense.

"Maybe. I don't know." Though afraid of his response, I slowly pulled my gaze from the computer monitor to peer at him.

A couple strolling the hallway entered our little corner. Spencer stood and blocked my laptop screen from their view.

"Oh, sorry. Didn't mean to interrupt," the man's voice stated.

"No apology needed," Spencer replied cheerfully.

The pair meandered farther down the hall, apparently wanting their privacy, too.

Spencer continued to watch them as they disappeared. "Polly,

I'm getting a bad feeling about all of this. Promise you'll wait for me before you question anyone else."

His protectiveness warmed me. I shook my head then pushed from the chair and stood to stretch. "That won't work. I'm getting pretty good at this questioning thing."

"You've got a method, have you?" He put his hands on his hips, emphasizing that he didn't believe me—a challenge to be sure. But then he winked.

My knees felt like jelly. Or was it Jell-O? I could never remember. "Yes, and I don't want you to mess with it." I shut down my laptop, gluing my eyes to the screen.

"At least allow me to be close enough to hear if you scream."

The concern in his voice drew my gaze. "You're serious?"

He quirked a brow. "I always am."

Was there a double meaning in his reply? The dry throat sensation returned as I pondered his earlier words and his kiss to my forehead. . .a promise of more between us.

"First we have to find the housekeeper." The room began to swim, tilting unsteadily to the right.

"That's easy enough. Find the housekeeping cart—Polly, are you all right?"

I swayed, my vision fuzzy. The next thing I knew, I was sitting on the small sofa, Spencer's strong hands gripping my shoulders. His face was near as he formed words. What was he saying?

"Are you all right?"

I shook my head to clear my mind. "Yes. I'm fine. I'm not sure what happened." Nothing tilted at the moment. Spencer's lips were dangerously close to mine.

"You fainted."

"What? No I didn't. I just got a little dizzy. It must be the altitude." I looked away from him. He released his grip, allowing me to slump against the cushion as he took a seat next to me.

"When did you last eat? You didn't eat lunch, I noticed."

"I don't remember. Look, we don't have time for this non-sensical fainting or dizziness, whatever it is. Let's go find the housekeeper." I had to escape his proximity.

Spencer rose from the sofa as though he sensed my discomfort. I hope he didn't misunderstand me, but what could I say? *I want you to kiss me, just not here.*

I gathered my laptop and camera. I had a hunch my time with the rangers would come soon. Romance should be the last thing on my mind.

We deposited my laptop in my room, keeping a sharp eye out for the housekeeper and a vending machine. Then we headed down the hall and around the corner. The crime-scene tape still blocked the room where Alec was murdered.

The housekeeper shouldn't have been in the room. Part of me thought all I needed to do was show the ranger my photos and that would be enough for him to question her. But another part wanted to talk to her myself. Though I couldn't imagine what other circumstances would cause me to investigate a crime, I might have enjoyed playing detective if Mom weren't a potential suspect. I felt a love-hate relationship developing around the whole idea of amateur sleuthing.

We ended up in the lobby, and I had no clear direction except the comfy-looking chair that called to me from a far, secluded corner. Spencer in my wake, I strode over and plopped down. "Look, maybe we should just go our separate ways for now.

Except if you find the housekeeper first, come and get me. I want to be the one to question her. Is that a deal?"

"It's not a deal unless I get something out of it."

"Okay, so I used the wrong word. How about this: I want to question her alone. Come and get me if you find her." A dry, sardonic tone I didn't mean escaped with the words.

"Say, you're getting cheeky. I'm not sure I like this new side of you." He jammed his hands in his pockets and quirked a half-sided grin.

When his left dimple showed up, my stomach flip-flopped, making me wonder where I would be when this weekend ended. Would I be bereft and heartbroken because Spencer had gotten under my skin again and then gone home, leaving me behind?

"I'm sorry, I shouldn't have snapped. I'm just. . .tired." And lightheaded to boot.

"Let me rephrase then, too. How about dinner tonight? Just you and me. There are certain things I want to discuss with you."

Even though expectancy rushed through me, there was still Mom to consider. She had to eat, too, and I couldn't keep leaving her. I looked at my watch. "It's almost two thirty." A lot could happen between now and dinnertime. Certain I'd forgotten something, panic chased my thoughts as I tried to remember. "Hey, aren't we supposed to have some sort of rehearsal for the wedding? Isn't that customary?"

Spencer groaned. "You're absolutely right. With everything that's happened, I'd forgotten."

"Help me out a little?"

Spencer eyed me, clearly not liking my sarcastic tone.

"Sorry, Polly." He tugged a slip of paper from his pocket.

"Conrad slipped this to me at breakfast this morning. Wedding rehearsal, four o'clock, in the Chamber Room."

Rene had been upset this morning about Spencer being taken for questioning. Still, I couldn't believe she'd forgotten to tell me. I was just about to grouse about it when the redheaded housekeeper came through a door behind the reception desk.

"There she is. I'm going after her."

Spencer touched my arm and whispered, "Be careful. And remember, I'll be nearby."

The housekeeper marched across the polished wood floor with purpose, heading in the opposite direction from where we sat. I hurried to catch her. She entered a hallway and stopped in front of the first door on the left. Gripping the doorknob, she looked around and saw me striding toward her, though still at a distance. I smiled and raised my hand to indicate I wanted to speak to her.

She ducked into the room. I quickened my pace and crossed the lobby near the registration desk, careful not to run into tourists coming and going with bags and children. When I arrived at the door she'd gone through, I read the large black letters that spelled ACCOUNTING OFFICE.

Here goes nothing. I opened the door and saw two women sitting behind computers.

One of them, a middle-aged woman, with glasses and brown hair cut short like a man's, looked up at me. "May I help you?"

"Yes, I'm looking for, um. . ." Mortified that I didn't know the housekeeper's name, I coughed and cleared my throat. "The housekeeper." *Idiot, idiot.*

Her smile became sympathetic. "I'm sorry, ma'am. This isn't housekeeping. Try the basement."

"The woman I want to speak with came in here." I tried to infuse my voice with more confidence this time.

The other woman, who resembled a Barbie doll, looked completely out of place in the rustic lodge, let alone the accounting office. I reminded myself that judging a book by its cover was never a good thing, and all that.

They shared a glance, then Barbie spoke. "There's no one in here but us."

"She was just here. I saw her come through the door."

The first woman flattened her lips then reached for the phone. I could guess what she was about to do. They thought I was crazy, and with a killer on the loose, this didn't look good.

"I'm sorry, I must be mistaken." I couldn't believe they were actually hiding her. Before I backed through the door, I heard a toilet flush, coming from a door in the back of the office. I smirked at the women then left the office.

I could wait. She had to come out eventually.

I leaned against the wall outside the office. After fifteen minutes, I wondered how long I should wait. The stairwell to the basement was located to my left at the end of the hall. A look to my right reassured me Spencer remained on the other side of the lobby with his nose in a newspaper. I wasn't sure from this distance, but I thought he glanced at me. I heard a door open near the stairwell. With a quick look in that direction, I saw a flash of red hair exiting through the door.

Somehow she'd gotten out of the office without coming through the door where I patiently waited. I rushed to follow her, thinking how ridiculous this had become. She had to be running from me. But why? We'd both shared a common experience.

She'd probably heard the rumor about *that photographer*. If only I could leave my camera behind. But it was too late—she'd already seen me with it.

I tried the door. Locked. I wanted to kick it in. Though sleuthing was a new pastime for me, I wasn't about to attempt breaking and entering. Besides, I had no way to disengage the lock, no credit card or sharp instrument like they used in the movies. The stairwell held new appeal, reminding me of the office woman's suggestion to visit the basement, where housekeeping was located.

As I went through the door to the basement, I hoped Spencer was close behind. The word "basement" brought with it all sorts of unimaginable horrors, images of torturous death and interminable darkness. After all, a dungeon was, in reality, the basement in a castle. This was the part in those scary movies where people yelled, "Don't do it! Don't go down there!"

I finally understood what drove the characters to march or creep inadequately armed into dark and sinister places. Stupid or not, I had to go. I had to find out.

My shoes echoed in the stairwell as I descended. So much for a stealthy approach. When I reached the basement, I found it alive with activity, bright light, and warm relief. To my mental sticky note, right under where I'd written "take up running," I added "stop watching old horror movies."

Still, I had, in fact, seen a dead body and was investigating a murder. I could be a little paranoid.

A young man pushed a cart filled with dirty sheets and towels past me into the laundry room containing giant washers and dryers. I saw no one I recognized, nor did anyone acknowledge me. Disappointed, I strolled to the other end of the corridor and into a restroom.

I almost collided with the housekeeper, whose eyes widened as she drew a fearful breath. We both repelled backward like opposing magnets, which positioned me against the door. She was trapped. She knew it and backed into the corner on cue as if we'd rehearsed this scene from a B movie of the worst kind. With scraggly hair and shadowed eyes, her face was a contortion of suppressed emotions.

A ticking bomb came to mind.

"Why are you running from me?" That wasn't a very tactical question, but I'd built up a lot of frustration, too.

"Why were you after me?"

I tried to remain serious, but laughter burst from my lips. Her gaping look made me wonder if I'd sounded maniacal. "Look, I'm not after you. I just wanted to talk, that's all."

"About what? I don't even know you."

"True. But we shared an awful experience. Let me introduce myself. I'm Polly Perkins." I stuck out my hand.

She hesitated before shaking it. "I'm Hillary Jennings."

Her name had a familiar ring to it. "Now that that's out of the way, how have you been doing? I mean, it's not every day you discover a body." I inwardly cringed. That wasn't the way to phrase it. For all I knew, she discovered bodies all the time.

"No, it's not." She turned her head slightly but kept suspicious eyes on me. "Look, I know who you are. You're that, that—"

"That photographer." Emphasis on *that*. "Yes, I've heard the rumors."

"Well, I'm not sure who you think you are, investigating and all, but I don't have to answer questions or talk to you."

I sighed. She'd forced my hand. "No, you don't have to talk to me. Instead, you can tell the authorities why you were in Alec's room today."

"What are you talking about?" Her widened eyes swept past me as if searching for a way out.

Now would be a good time to take advice from the old adage about cornered animals, but I couldn't remember what it was. I hoped Spencer had followed me to the basement. "I took a picture of you in Alec's room today. What were you doing there if they're still gathering forensic evidence?"

"I. . .I was searching for the necklace I lost the day I cleaned that room."

It was my turn to be suspicious. She wasn't wearing any jewelry now or any makeup. In my years in the portrait business, I had a good sense of who wore jewelry and who didn't. There was no science to it, just a feeling. "It must have been very precious to have risked being caught in that room today. Can you describe it?"

"It was. . . It had. . ." Her eyes darted to my necklace. "A cross."

Dizziness threatened me again, urging me to hurry. I forged on. "You weren't looking for a necklace. Now tell me why you were there." I'd never felt comfortable confronting anyone, and my bold words now disturbed me. But I heard in them something else—a warning to be careful. If misconstrued, things could be interpreted that I was after something in Alec's room, too, and that I'd killed him to get it.

She covered her face and began to sob as she tried to communicate, not unlike what I'd seen my mother do earlier.

"I didn't kill him. I swear." Her bawls grew until they sounded like howling. "I was having an affair with Alec."

After what seemed like thirty minutes but was probably only thirty seconds, she regained control. "Please, please don't tell my husband." She grabbed a Kleenex from the wall box and blew her nose.

How could I do that? I didn't even know who he was. "I won't tell your husband if you'll share with me what you were looking for today and why you had Alec's handkerchief in your hand the day of his murder."

The door swooshed open from behind, bumping me forward. A large woman shoved her way into the restroom. When she saw Hillary, she eyed me suspiciously. "You all right, Hillary? This lady bothering you?" She put her hands on her hips.

"I'm fine, thanks, May. I was just leaving."

Hillary slipped out without answering my question. I'd have to chase her down again. That is, if I got the chance.

May stood in my way. "Say, you're *that photographer*."

"Yes, I suppose I am."

"You better hope you can defend yourself, snooping around like you're doin'." She straightened to her full height.

I pushed past her large frame and eased the door open enough to slide through. Was she warning me, too? I hurried from the basement, my head spinning with all that Hillary had said. I still didn't have answers about the handkerchief or what she'd been searching for today, but I had something else. She'd had an affair with Alec. I told her that I wouldn't tell her husband. And I wouldn't. But this was definitely something for the authorities. They could tell him.

My spirits sank when I discovered that Spencer was nowhere in sight. He'd either given up on me or had lost me on my jaunt to the basement. I pulled the small memory card from my camera and strode through the lobby in hopes of finding one of the several rangers or detectives roaming the place.

While I wasn't giving up my private investigation, time was running out. They needed to see the photographs I'd taken. The chief ranger strode through the lobby doors directly toward me. I smiled, though I was nervous. He stopped in front of me and nodded.

Before he could say anything, I blurted, "I have something you might want to see. I took photographs the day Alec died, but I've taken other possibly incriminating pictures. In fact, I took one today of the housekeeper Hillary Jennings."

"Hillary Jennings, you say?" Rangers must be trained to hide their emotions, because his face remained expressionless, even though I detected something threatening in his voice. "Ms. Perkins, I came here to take you in for questioning. I've discovered that you had a reason to hate Alec Gordon. Now I think you're attempting to divert my attention away from you. Keep me from questioning you."

He tugged the card from my rigid hand. I stood frozen and speechless.

"I don't suppose you know that Hillary Jennings is my wife."

CHAPTER TWELVE

The ranger station, resembling a large log home, as one might expect, bustled with activity as tourists visited the information center and the store cluttered with national park paraphernalia. What looked like a small infirmary stood apart from it on the other side of the parking lot.

All this I saw as I climbed out of Ranger Jennings's fully equipped, four-wheel drive SUV, adorned to leave no doubt of his law-enforcement authority. Too bad the nearest boulder was too far away for me to duck behind and hide my embarrassment. Why couldn't he have one of those sedans I'd seen some of the other rangers driving? They didn't draw attention and weren't nearly as intimidating.

Ranger Jennings took my elbow to escort me from the parking lot through a side entrance. I'd tried not to panic, though most of my calm and friendly posturing depleted while we drove the three miles to the station in silence.

He left me in a stuffy room with a table and two chairs. It looked like where they question suspects on a police-detective television series. I'd been expecting to sit in his office so I could browse photographs of his family and friends or distract myself with perusing his paperwork or mail when he wasn't looking—a wrong thing to do, but why hide the truth of what people did? Though I'd lost my appetite earlier in the day, my stomach growled uncontrollably, probably explaining the lightheadedness I'd contended with for the last couple of hours. Concentration would be difficult.

Clues were strewn all over the gray carpet of my mind, driving me nuts. I made an attempt to organize them before he returned. I'd told Hillary Jennings that I wouldn't tell her husband about her affair with Alec Gordon, thinking that I would tell the ranger instead. How could I have known that her husband and the ranger were the same person?

Things were about to get tricky. Ranger Jennings already believed I was trying to distract him by pointing the finger at his wife. She could always add to his suspicious opinion about me with her story, "That crazy photographer chased me into the bathroom and cornered me."

If asked, how could I deny it?

The door swung open to reveal the man himself. I'd held on to a small hope that someone else would interrogate me. Before sitting, he asked, "May I get you anything to drink?"

"A soda, please." The carbonation might help to curb my now-ravenous appetite.

"We're fresh out. How about coffee or water?"

"Coffee. French vanilla if you have it, please."

He got up and cracked the door to ask someone for water.

Sitting down, he answered my unspoken question. "Haven't got the fancy stuff. As I mentioned, we've learned that you had a previous relationship with Mr. Gordon. Why didn't you tell me about this when I questioned you before?"

"Because before, you asked me specifically what I'd seen regarding his body. Nothing more." I'd thought about my relationship with Alec since first running into him and even during the few moments of horror as I stared at his body. But I couldn't afford to think about it now. I might blurt out something that could be interpreted as motivation to commit a murder. Tiny beads of sweat erupted under my eyes.

Ranger Jennings nodded. I suspected he already knew the answer but was hoping to see my reaction. He looked at his notepad then back at me.

Thirty seconds without speaking during an interrogation is a long time.

I cleared my throat. Maybe he hoped to torture me with silence. How long could I hold out? There was a tap on the door, then it opened. A big-boned woman clad in what I'd term a cute ranger dress suit stepped into the room and set a glass of water on the table. I nodded my thanks, still not breaking the silence, and smiled at Ranger Jennings.

"Tell me about your previous relationship with the victim."

A tiny voice inside murmured that I should get a lawyer. I shunned the thought, because I wasn't guilty. "Can I know how you found out about it?" I took a long drink of water to hide the surprise of my boldness—since I began sleuthing, it started popping up everywhere, including unlikely and inappropriate places.

He inclined his head. "Your mother told me."

Mom?

Water spewed from my lips. "Oh! I'm so sorry. I'll clean it up." I jumped from the table and spun around. "Where are tissues or napkins? Anything?"

Ranger Jennings wiped himself off with his handkerchief. Still no frown.

No emotion. "Sit down, Ms. Perkins. We'll get it later. Now, could you please answer my question?"

How could he question me while staring at the mess I'd made? Remembering I had a tissue, I tugged it from my pocket. Unfortunately Alec Gordon's business card came with it and dropped to the table—a neon sign reflecting red across my face.

With a heavy sigh, I lowered myself into the chair. "There's nothing much to say. We went to school together, that's all." Another sip of water allowed me to watch Ranger Jennings over the rim of my glass. In return, he watched me while he toyed with the business card. A disastrous thought occurred to me. Had Mom also told him about the accident?

"What can you tell me about the accident?"

She'd done it. Rolling my head back, I stared at the ceiling. Hurt and frustration flooded my thoughts. I had to focus, ignore the fact that Mom had told the ranger things she should have left to me. "Alec was driving the car that killed my best friend."

God forgive me, I had wished he'd died instead.

Here I was, at that pivotal moment I'd worried about—would a crime committed by my heart make me a suspect, make me guilty in the eyes of the chief ranger of Caldera National Park? Not knowing what else he wanted in answer, I wasn't about to offer how the accident made me feel.

"How did that make you feel?"

"What are you, a psychiatrist?" I shoved from the table and paced the room. "That was years ago. How do you think it made me feel?"

"You tell me." His expression remained void of emotion. Would he be offended if I photographed him during our session?

"It doesn't matter how it made me feel. I didn't kill Alec Gordon. If I had wanted him dead, had intended to kill him, I would have done it years ago." I pressed my lips together. I'd said too much.

Ranger Jennings wrote at length in his notebook. I took a seat across from him again and tapped my fingers on the table. His eyes darted to my hand then back to his notebook. A slight crease in his brow appeared. Aha, an irritation. He could be made to show emotion. I took my camera out of the case and fiddled with it. Could I manage a shot of him?

"So I can't be accused of not asking you a specific question, is there anything else you know about the victim you can share with me?"

Ouch. His question had opened the door for me to tell him his wife had been having an affair with Alec Gordon. So she said. She'd confided in me, but would it be my word against hers? At this point, how could I trust her to take the high road?

I'd given him the photographs and hoped he was smart enough to figure it out. Otherwise, what would I tell him? *George had given Alec a dirty look? One of the tourists lied about knowing him? Your boat tour guide is morbid? Your wife, who was supposedly cleaning the room when she found Alec, held his handkerchief in her hand?* So what?

Because I'd given him the memory card, I didn't have an extra one on me and couldn't take a snapshot of him anyway. Feeling more like an idiot than ever, I stuffed my camera back in its case. "I think everything I have to tell you about the victim, as you call him, is on my camera's memory card, which I already gave you. I've been taking photographs since I arrived. I encourage you to look at them."

He wrote more in his notepad. I had the distinct impression he wasn't taking me seriously. If he didn't discover his wife's relationship with Alec on his own, what would I do? It occurred to me that he might want to protect her. What if he destroyed the memory card?

Ranger Jennings returned me to the lodge, informing me he would probably need to question me again. In other words, *don't leave*. That was fine with me until Monday rolled around. Then, I would need to get back to my business on the coast. By the time I arrived in my room, I was shaken, drained, and starved. The rangers could at least have offered me a Twinkie for my trouble. Wanting an extra measure of safety, I bolted the door behind me.

Considering how I'd last left Spencer—glancing at me from the lobby while I tracked down the housekeeper—he might call for a search party if I didn't contact him soon. But I couldn't think straight. A glance at the clock told me it was nearing five. Dinner couldn't come soon enough. Remembering that I'd stuffed the side pocket of one of my bags with a few protein bars, I opened the closet to look for them.

Something on the floor caught my foot.

Hillary Jennings was cradled there, motionless. A long scream came from somewhere—it seemed outside of my body.

"Oh Lord, please not again." I dropped to my knees to examine her, shake her to life, barely noticing the pounding on the door. The knob jiggled.

"Hillary, are you alive? Wake up!" Tears streamed down my face as I tried to find a pulse. My hands shook too much.

"Polly! What's going on? Let me in." Spencer yelled through the door.

I unbolted the door and opened it. It felt like reverse déjà vu. I pointed to the closet. "It's Hillary, the housekeeper. . ." I slumped against the edge of the bed, trembling.

Spencer knelt next to her, looking for signs of life.

"Is she. . .is she—"

"She's alive. Call 911 or whatever it is you call in this place."

I called the operator, uncertain how things worked in a national park in the middle of nowhere. Within minutes, medics arrived, lifting Hillary out of the closet onto a stretcher. I wondered if we should have already eased her from the awkward position. We'd left her, I suppose, so the authorities could see her as I found her. I now saw how heartless the decision had been.

While they were moving her, Spencer wrapped his arm around my shoulders. "We might have hurt her, had we moved her, love," he said, with a quick and tender peck on my cheek.

The kiss and endearment—something new from him—would have made me weak in the knees at any other time. I knew he was doing his best to comfort me. In return, I offered a wan smile. "I know."

Hillary moaned and woke up, complaining about her head. She tried to climb off the stretcher, claiming she didn't want to go to the hospital. The medics, assisted by two rangers, held her firmly as they wheeled her through the door. I wanted to collapse. Seeing someone on the closet floor twice now had reduced me to rubble, a woman whose tattered emotions lay in ruins.

I held strong until they were completely out the door and prayed silently the two rangers would leave with them as well. It struck me odd that Ranger Jennings, Hillary's husband, had not come. Although I was worried for her, I was afraid of what he would think about me finding her in my room.

Spencer made to close the door against the madness in the corridor, but a familiar uniform stepped into the doorway. In no mood to answer more questions, I slumped onto the small love seat. One of the two rangers who'd answered the emergency had returned.

"Ma'am, can you tell me what happened here?" He stood poised, pen and pad ready.

"You're not going to take me to the station?"

Young and seemingly inexperienced, he cleared his throat. "Not unless you want me to."

Spencer stepped between us. "Look, she's drained and needs rest. And I suspect something to eat. Can't this wait?"

The ranger's tense shoulders dropped. "If you can just tell me what happened, I can take your statement now. In case you hadn't noticed, we have our hands full with this murder investigation.

I don't want to have to take you to the station either."

Had he just arrived from Mars? Didn't he know of my involvement? Ranger Jennings would have come unglued—in his own unemotional way—to find his wife in my closet, considering I was already on his list of interesting people.

Still, I was relieved at the ranger's consideration. I explained that I'd come back to my room then opened my closet. That was all.

He clicked his pen when he finished writing. "Is there anything missing in your room or out of place? Did you see anyone suspicious in the hall?"

I glanced around my room. "I don't see anything out of place, no. Honestly, I'd just come in. I might discover something missing later. And I didn't notice anyone."

He jotted more in his notebook before giving me his attention. "I'm sure we'll have more questions later. Don't leave until you talk to us first."

Yeah. Yeah. "Thanks." I tried to smile brightly at him. I'd been given a reprieve—at least for the moment. *Thank you for that, Lord.*

Spencer looked at me and shrugged then directed his attention to the ranger. "Say, how's that murder investigation getting on? Caught anyone yet? Do we need to be worried?"

I couldn't believe his audacity, but he apparently thought since the ranger didn't realize who I was, he'd take advantage of it.

The ranger lowered his voice. "I'm not supposed to discuss the case, but I assure you, we're close to an arrest."

Though I'd already heard that news from Mom, hearing it again left me stunned anyway. I hoped they'd not decided to pin the murder on her. Or me for that matter.

Spencer shut the door when the ranger left then crossed his arms, leaning against the door. "Well, that was a bit odd."

"Yes." It was all too bizarre.

I stared through Spencer, the words hanging in my mind.

Too bizarre.

How strange that Hillary confessed she'd had an affair with Alec, then while her ranger husband questioned me, someone left her in my closet as though dead, like Alec.

Things were not falling into place. I had the strange feeling that by attempting to solve the murder, I was cluttering the case—like some sort of distorted, self-fulfilling prophecy. I'd seen too many movies in which the attempt to prevent a prediction coming true actually caused it to come true.

And not just in movies. This was becoming all too familiar, reminding me of the awful weekend Brandon went missing. A terrible foreboding had nagged me all week long. When Brandon made plans to drive to Seattle for a business trip a few days early in order to see his mother, I feared my apprehension was somehow related to his trip. Instead of giving it to the Lord, I'd convinced him to stay home for the weekend, to go sailing instead. He'd not returned from the sailing trip.

So now I had to wonder, had my questioning Hillary led her to my room?

Before her mysteriously absent husband got to her, I had to know.

I opened the door and pushed Spencer out. "I'll meet you, say, in an hour at the restaurant inside the lodge."

At his stunned expression, I stood on my toes and pecked his cheek. "All is well. See you in a bit."

His mouth hung open as though he had something to tell me, wanted to protest, but I closed the door on him. I felt bad, but I didn't think Hillary would reveal anything with him around. She might not be as open if I didn't come alone.

I couldn't think without nourishment. I scrambled to the closet for those protein bars. Finding two bars—one of them crushed, but no matter—I ate them as I gathered my thoughts.

Why had Hillary been in my room? And who had put her in my closet?

I knew what I had to do next. Before leaving my room, I grabbed a new memory card, replacing the one I'd given to Ranger Jennings, and deposited it in the appropriate camera slot.

—

As I drove the three miles to the small infirmary where I hoped they'd taken Hillary, a thought occurred to me. By going to question her like this, I was becoming entangled even deeper in the investigation. So far, my amateur interrogations, however fruitful, had been—if I were honest with myself—hit-or-miss. But now my actions were calculated.

Pulling into the parking lot, I made for the far side of the infirmary, out of view from the ranger station. My greatest fear at the moment was running into Ranger Jennings. Once he learned the news concerning his wife, he was sure to be at her side.

Then he would come looking for me.

I took a step from my car and paused. Was I attempting an impossible task? *Lord, please don't let me run into him.*

I had to consider the possibility that Hillary hadn't come to my room of her own volition, that she'd been dragged or forced into my room, no matter how far-fetched it seemed. The way things were going, nothing would surprise me. In essence, discovering Hillary in my closet had increased my DEFCON readiness to level 2, just under maximum readiness. When or how it happened, I wasn't sure, but somehow I'd learned to cope differently, better. I no longer needed my camera for therapy, even when the world of murder and mayhem had finally caught up with Mom and me.

As an unwilling captive, I had to find an escape—for both of us.

I strode toward the glass double doors of the main entrance to the infirmary, questions slamming my mind. Had Hillary come to my room to tell me something? A warning, perhaps?

Ignoring my sweating palms, I pushed through the door, not knowing what I'd find. A desk sat in the corner of the small reception area. Voices came from beyond a wide double door. One of them was definitely Hillary's. I strode forward, noticing as I entered that the room was equipped for only limited medical services.

The discussion stopped. Hillary gasped when she saw me then threw her legs over the edge of the examination table and sat up, ignoring the protests of the man giving her medical attention.

"No, please don't get up." Sorry for startling Hillary, guilt flooded me. What kind of person was I to prey upon an injured person?

She eased herself back against the pillow, but her expression remained strained.

The man nodded at me then looked back at Hillary. "I'll leave you two alone for a minute. But I still insist that you go to the hospital." With that, he exited the room.

Sympathy flooded me, but I had to stick to my purpose. "I'm so sorry you're hurt. What did the doctor say?"

"I might have a concussion."

"You're going to the hospital, right?"

She shook her head, wincing. "No, I can't leave now." She scrunched her brows.

"Have you talked to your husband about what happened in Alec's room?" I waited for her reply. Had he gotten to her first? I was afraid if he talked to her before I did, anything she'd planned to tell me would be lost in the melee, especially if he'd looked at the photos.

"No, he's gone to town, something to do with the investigation."

"I'm sorry he's not here to be with you."

She looked away, but I'd caught the hint of moisture in her eyes. I felt like a heel for hoping he wouldn't have come yet. Were my true colors showing now that I faced pressure? Had I turned into a monster?

"Finding you in my closet like that was a shock. Especially after—"

"I know. I was there; you don't have to remind me." She released a slow breath.

"Hillary, I'm just glad you weren't in the same condition as Alec. Did you see who it was?"

She placed a finger against her lips and motioned me to close the double doors. Her voice quivered. "I was in your room cleaning when someone hit me over the head."

"But I didn't see a cart outside my room." And then it hit me. I hadn't seen a cart outside the room when I responded to

Hillary's screams and saw Alec in the closet either.

"All right, I'm in deep enough already. I came to your room to talk to you. When you didn't answer, I let myself in to wait for you. I'm sorry. It's just that. . .I'm scared."

Looking at Hillary now, I could see some resemblance between us. We were about the same height and had similar auburn hair. I wondered if I'd been the intended victim.

She sniffled and reached for a tissue. It seemed I had that effect on her. "Did you tell my husband about my affair with Alec?"

"No, I didn't. But I might have. I had no idea that Ranger Jennings was your husband."

A short laugh spilled from her. "That figures. In fact, I'm not sure it would make much difference to him. His career is all-important. He might even try to gloss over that little detail, once he learns of my affair, to protect himself. But. . .why didn't you tell him?" Her eyes held gratitude, which made me wince at the truth.

"I gave him the photographs I've taken since being at the park. He's probably smart enough to figure things out, don't you think? Like the fact that you weren't in Alec's room to clean? But even if he doesn't, I hope you'll tell him."

"I can't. I won't."

"So, why did you need to see me?" I prayed silently that she had nothing to do with Alec's murder.

She played with her tissue, her features steeped in a deep frown. "There's a murderer out there, and I'm scared. I need your help. Since you're trying to find out who it is on your own, I want to help. I'll tell you everything I know. But I'll deny every bit if you try to tell the authorities. If I can make it through this mess without my husband finding out. . ."

I sucked in a breath. Hadn't I just encouraged her to tell the truth? There was more to the reason she was hiding the affair from her husband, I sensed.

"Alec had a diamond ring he claimed was worth twenty grand." She dabbed at her eyes and spoke through tears. "I. . . thought he meant to propose, which was ludicrous. I'm still married. But no. He wanted us to travel to Europe!"

I snatched another tissue to replace the one she'd shredded and handed it to her.

"Thanks." She took the fresh one and tossed the old one in the small receptacle next to the bed. "I'd already made up my mind to end the affair. In fact, that's why I met with him that day. But he wouldn't hear of it. My refusal to go with him made him crazy. I'd never seen him like that. He said he planned to leave the country and demanded that I leave my husband." She covered her face. "I never meant for this to happen. For things to go this far."

I held the box of tissues out to her. Once she regained her composure, she continued. "My refusal sent him into a tirade. He threatened to expose our affair. I told him it was over and tried to leave the room, but he overpowered me." Hillary fell into sobs.

Unfortunately I believed her. It sounded just like the Alec I knew from years ago. My best friend had planned to break things off with him the very night he'd crashed his car, causing her death.

I patted her shoulder, unsure how to console her. I hated seeing her relive this. Should I be the one to hear this confession? Surely Ranger Jennings needed to hear it. But she'd already told me she would deny everything.

She blew her nose long and hard then took a deep breath. "At that moment, I thought he would kill me. You should have seen the anger in his eyes. I struggled and managed to grab a lamp. Normally it would have been fastened to the table, but we'd just replaced it, and maintenance hadn't made it to that room yet. Thank God, or I might not be here. I hit him over the head, and he let go of me. I was so scared that I ran out of the room."

"You left? But how did he get in the closet?"

She stopped crying and looked at me then shook her head before wincing again. "I don't know how he got in the closet. I was frantic about what I'd done and went back to see if he was going to be all right. That's when I found him in the closet. I remembered the ring and searched his pockets. I didn't find anything but his handkerchief. I thought he was just unconscious and felt for a pulse. There wasn't one."

She'd looked for his ring to steal it? I let the question go for now. "And that's when you screamed, and I came into the room."

She nodded.

I covered my eyes. What a tangled mess. She'd just confessed everything to me so that I would have more to go on. Now I would be the one in trouble if I didn't tell the rangers everything she'd told me. I would be facing her denial and a chief ranger who, according to Hillary, always protected his career and, on top of that, already thought I was trying to divert attention from myself.

My shoulders drooped. I turned my thoughts back to considering all she'd told me.

I didn't need to look through my camera lens to see that she was telling the truth. That meant one thing. Whoever murdered

Alec had the ring. In my limited experience at sleuthing, I figured: Find the ring, find the murderer. Alec had scammed Mom out of a large sum of money. Add the value of the ring to that, and he had enough to flee the country. I couldn't help but believe he'd scammed more than Mom, though, because seventy thousand dollars wouldn't last all that long.

Somehow I had to convince Hillary to go to the authorities. "Look, you've got to tell your husband all of this. Do you know how angry he'll be when he finds out you kept this from him? I mean, even besides your affair—all this other information is vital to the investigation."

"I can't tell him any of it. Don't you see? Telling him what really happened means I'd have to tell him about the affair. And if I tell them I hit Alec with the lamp, I'd be all but admitting to murder. What if they don't believe me? All I was trying to do was make him let go of me. When he fell on the floor, I made sure he was alive—he was still breathing—and he wasn't bleeding at all. Thank goodness I didn't kill him. Still, I was afraid of him, afraid of what might happen if I called for help, so I left him there." A sob escaped Hillary.

I touched her arm. "Think of it like this: You're alive. God has given you a second chance to do the right thing. Tell your husband the truth."

Voices sounded outside the infirmary, signifying someone could soon enter the reception area. Hillary quickly cleaned up the tissues, and I could tell she was trying to compose herself, but her eyes were red and swollen. "You'd better leave now. And. . .be careful."

I nodded and opened the door.

Ranger Jennings loomed large in the doorway, anger growing in his features. Every time I saw him, he revealed a little more emotion.

Before he could speak, I said, "I came by to see how she's doing." Did he know I'd found her in my closet? Would he think I'd done it?

"I know what you were up to, and I doubt it has anything to do with my wife's condition. I'm warning you to cease and desist your interference in this case. You're going to ruin my investigation. Before I let that happen, I'll cite you for obstruction of justice. Do you understand?"

I gulped and nodded then hurried past him. To my horror, he followed me, shutting the door behind him. He lowered his voice to a whisper. "Oh, and don't run too far. I'll need to question you about finding my wife in your closet."

"But. . .but someone already did that."

"I know. But I still want to talk to you. Right now, I need to make sure she's all right." Something in his tone wavered. I suspected he was broken up about Hillary but didn't want to show it.

She'd just given me the explosive compounds to make a very large bomb. That is, if I were making bombs. I hoped she would tell her husband, because if I didn't, I feared that would be considered withholding evidence.

CHAPTER THIRTEEN

Irushed through the doors of the restaurant and dashed past the maitre d', hoping I hadn't stood Spencer up yet again. He sat alone at a table in the far corner, looking anything but relaxed. As soon as he spotted me, he smiled and rose, his concerned expression transforming into exuberance.

Always the gentleman, he pulled out a chair for me. "Good of you to come, Polly. I hope you got some rest."

I wished I'd taken a moment outside the restaurant doors to steady my breath following my mad rush to meet him. After swallowing half the glass of water next to my table setting, I said, "Sorry I'm late."

"I'm just glad you made it. I can't help but notice this is becoming a habit with you."

Uncertain how to tell him what I'd been up to and that it hadn't been restful, I was glad when I remembered Mom. "There's so much going on. But first, if you wouldn't mind, I need to call Mom. I know you said you wanted to talk about something—just you and me—but I'd like for her to eat with us. I haven't seen much of her."

He gave a sympathetic nod.

I made to stand.

Spencer gently grabbed my arm, indicating he wanted me to stay seated. I slid back into my chair, and he placed his hand over mine. The simple gesture sent my heart racing. Somehow, I had to control my emotions. I forced my thoughts back to the circumstances. "What is it, Spencer?"

"There's something I'd like to tell you now. Earlier today when I came to your room, I had planned to tell you. . . ." He stared at his hand, still covering mine. "Not sure how to break this, but we went ahead with the rehearsal without you."

"What?" Shame filled me. What was the matter with me? Why couldn't I handle a murder investigation and being interrogated by the ranger as a possible suspect, all on top of wedding preparations? I had completely forgotten about the rehearsal, but then again, I was being questioned. Would they have released me to go to the rehearsal?

Spencer finally pulled his hand from mine. "When you dashed after the housekeeper, I waited and read my paper, watching the door you'd entered, waiting for you to come out. You were gone a long time, and I got worried. I was just getting up to follow you when I saw you come into the lobby and run into Ranger Jennings. You left with him. I presume he questioned you?"

Spencer gazed at me, waiting for a response. I nodded.

"When you didn't return in time for the rehearsal, Rene decided to go ahead without you. She said you'd only be taking the photographs and weren't a necessary part of the rehearsal."

I drew in a deep breath, uncertain which I felt more—weariness or disappointment.

Spencer frowned. "I'm sorry, Polly."

"It's not your fault. I'll live. Now, give me a minute to call Mom. I'll be right back, I promise." I shook my head as I got up. If only I'd actually had a chance to rest, maybe I wouldn't feel so confused and overwhelmed. He was right, after all. There wasn't a big need for me to attend the rehearsal.

"Uh, Polly. Where are you going?" Spencer tossed his cell on the table.

"Oh, right." I slid back into the seat across from him and picked up his phone, wondering about the number to call. "What about Conrad and Rene? You could invite them to dinner. Or do they already have plans?"

"A guided tour of something. Not sure. They invited me, but I wanted to dine with you. It's all a bit awkward, isn't it?"

Unsure of what he meant, I gave him a questioning look.

"We're here for them, but they're never around."

I sighed. "I'm not sure I could handle an investigation and entertaining a pair of almost newlyweds."

He chuckled. "Right you are. Here, let me help you." He took the cell from me and pressed a button, handing the phone back to me.

After connecting with the main number, my call was transferred to Mom's room. With each ring, I worked to push aside my ire that she'd shared information about me with the ranger—after all, I only had one mother.

"Hello?"

"Mom, it's—"

"Oh, Polly! How did it go? I've been so worried about you."

How did everyone know I'd been questioned? I assumed Spencer had shared the news. "Mom, things went as well as could be expected. Listen, Spencer and I are in the restaurant for dinner. Would you like to join us?"

"Oh, heavens, no. I just came in from a jaunt not too long ago, and after the conversation with my lawyer—"

"What? When did you talk to a lawyer?" Panic swelled inside me. Had things escalated that much?

"Well, you don't think I plan to sit around while my money is used on some scam by a person who isn't even alive, do you? And I'm afraid all of this is too much for my stomach. In fact, I've got to let you go, or I won't make it to the bathroom." The phone line went dead.

I stared at the phone before setting it on the table in front of Spencer. Despite suffering with a stomach ailment—or spastic colon, as it was sometimes termed—Mom sounded better, more upbeat. And she'd taken the initiative to contact a lawyer. I hoped she wouldn't need a defense attorney.

Spencer watched me but said nothing.

"I'll be right back." I left him and headed to the ladies' room to splash water on my face, wash my hands, and gather my thoughts. When I looked at my reflection in the mirror, I wondered what Spencer saw in me. I was more of a wreck now than when I left the coast to come here, hoping for a refreshing weekend. I turned my head upside down to fluff my hair and give it some volume and applied some lip gloss I kept in my pocket.

Though I wasn't satisfied with my appearance for dinner with Spencer, it would have to do.

Back at the table, I sat down to a plate of Hawaiian chicken.

Spencer gave me a sheepish grin. "I took the liberty of ordering for you. I figured you'd be famished by the time you got here."

The protein bars I'd wolfed down earlier had quit for the day, and I was ravenous. "How did you know what I wanted?" I smirked, never doubting his answer.

"A wild guess, really."

"You're good." I grinned. I've always been afraid to try something new for fear I wouldn't like it and that it would be a waste of money. So I stick with my old favorite, even though I've forgotten at what point I'd first tried the pineapple-smothered chicken.

"I wish Mom could have joined us." Even though part of me knew that was true, the other part was glad I was alone with Spencer. I hoped he sensed that.

"I'm sorry, Polly." He reached across the table and took my hand, sending a wave of something warm and unexpected through me.

I looked at him and saw that he was sincere. "Thanks for your concern. I think she sounds much improved from earlier, but if it weren't for this investigation, I'd send her home so she could garden or do something therapeutic."

Spencer quirked the left side of his mouth—the smile I loved. But I could tell it lacked its usual brilliance and figured he was concerned about her, too. My mind was reeling with what Hillary had told me, but I kept it to myself until I knew what Spencer wanted to talk about.

"Look, Polly." He stared at the place setting in front of him. "I don't want what I have to say spoiled with thoughts of murder.

I think you've got too much on your mind. At least, much more on your mind than just me."

He put his hand to his mouth and frowned. "If it weren't for this wretched murder."

I searched his eyes, questioning. Had I understood him correctly? He'd alluded to something more between us earlier in the day, but I dared not hope. If I were reading his expression right and not just seeing what I wanted, he'd planned to talk about us tonight. It was everything I hoped, everything I feared—he'd hurt me before. I couldn't deny that he'd occupied my thoughts even while I searched for clues. If anything good could be said about this amateur investigation, it was that I was thankful for the distraction of a murder to solve.

I was the first to break eye contact, embarrassed by my thoughts. Though tempted by the hint of romance I saw in his eyes, I needed to remain cautious where Spencer Bradford was concerned. I toyed with my glass of water. "Yes, a murder does throw a wrench into things, doesn't it?" My stomach growled.

Spencer watched me savor my first bite and smiled. "It's funny, that."

"What? That I always eat the same thing?" Being near Spencer and basking in the romantic ambience, my appetite almost began to wane. Almost.

He grinned then stuck a forkful of chicken in his mouth.

"But I don't always eat the same thing. If I'm at an Italian restaurant, I eat lasagna."

I could tell by his expression that he wanted to laugh but couldn't. When he finished chewing, he wiped his mouth with his napkin. "The way the conversation's going, I could easily go right into what I want to discuss with you."

At that moment, I wished he would. "But you're not."

"No, too much is hanging over us. I want nothing of the sort when I. . ." He squinted and looked away in thought.

"Don't do that to me. Finish what you were going to say, please."

"Well, to complete the sentence would be to talk about what I'm trying not to talk about." He winked.

It was hard to be frustrated with Spencer—the guy could find humor in any situation. But he wouldn't find what I had to tell him next very funny. We finished eating in silence while I considered how to tell Spencer about Hillary's confession.

Spencer placed his napkin and utensils on his plate. "So, let's talk about our private investigation. Do you have any thoughts about why Hillary was in your closet?"

I sucked in a breath. What would he think when I told him what I'd done? But there was nothing for it. "It just so happens that I paid her a visit before coming here."

"You what?" He'd spoken much too loud, reminding me of Mom. He realized it, too, and lowered his voice. "Where?"

I didn't answer as he waved the waiter over and paid for the meal. I objected, but he wouldn't hear of me paying. Chivalrous as always.

He leaned in and whispered, "Let's take this conversation where we can be sure we're out of earshot."

It seemed like he was leaning and whispering a lot lately. I liked the nearness. "Good idea. But where?"

"The evening is still early. Let's take a stroll along the rim."

After I shared Hillary's story, we went round and round about whether or not Hillary was the murderer and had lied to me. I believed her. Spencer wasn't sure. Even if she had committed the crime, who had hit her over the head and put her in the closet? Or could she have staged it?

"I don't see how," Spencer said. "You did say they think she has a concussion, right? Say she'd gotten into the closet then hit herself over the head, which is hardly plausible. We would have seen whatever she used to hit herself with lying around."

A cool breeze gusted, making me pull my jacket tight. "Who knows when someone else will be discovered in a closet?"

Spencer tugged me to him and wrapped his arm around me, warming me to my toes. "Now, Polly, I think Alec was the target and not anyone else. Hillary was involved with Alec, so she became a target, too."

"I wonder if the rangers should claim she's dead to protect her?" I didn't mention the possibility that I'd been the intended victim, not Hillary.

Why did a murder have to occur on the weekend when I'd see Spencer again? How I wished he would just come out with whatever he had to say. But he was right. We didn't need anything hanging over us.

As we strolled back toward the lobby, Spencer and I went over all the possible clues we'd found, including what we knew about Emily.

"What's her name?"

"Who, Emily?"

"Yes, her. What's her real name?"

"Um. . .I don't know."

Eyes narrowed, he gave me his lopsided grin. "I'm disappointed in you. I thought you were a master sleuth."

"Oh, really, Mr. CSI." I considered asking him about with-holding information from the authorities. But I feared he would put an end to the sleuthing if I told him about Ranger Jennings's warning. I'd begun my search for the criminal with Mom as a possible suspect, and now I was one, too. But Hillary had added her name to the list when she'd asked for my help. She seemed truly scared. What would happen if she told no one what she knew, and I stopped working to solve the crime? I feared the worst—the real murderer would go free.

I jabbed Spencer with my elbow. "Well, here's one for you. Why don't you find out her real name and then see what you can discover about her? It was a mistake for her to insist I destroy any photos of her. She only made me curious about who she is."

"Obviously she thought it worth the risk, rather than see them pop up where they weren't supposed to. All right, I'm intrigued. I'll see what I can find out about her. But I need her *real name*."

We'd come to a stop in the lobby. Spencer made to plop down on one of the large, comfortable sofas.

"Hey, wait." I had an idea. "See that cute little blond receptionist over at the front desk?"

Spencer eyed me curiously. "This isn't one of those trick questions, is it?"

I laughed. "No, I'm serious. We need to discover what we can about the other guests. We could be missing something or someone here. I think you need to cozy up to the cute blond and find out what you can."

I think I caught him off guard big-time. Now it was his turn to laugh. "Surely you can't be serious. First, I don't see a cute blond. And second, I can't just saunter up to her and become

Prince Charming."

"Oh, but you sell yourself short. I thought all men thought highly of themselves." I reached up and finger combed his unruly hair. "Sorry, you just needed a little tweaking."

"In that case, shouldn't I take a shower and put on some cologne?"

I quirked a brow. "Didn't you already do that for me not an hour ago?" I took a deep breath. "I can still smell your cologne. You're fine. Besides, she'll love your British accent." A seed of doubt that this was a good idea began to niggle under my skin.

Spencer thought for a moment, postured in his signature position—elbow on arm, fingers across lip. He snapped his fingers. "I've got it. Let's stage an argument. A giant lover's quarrel, if you will." His face reddened slightly. "Hence she'll be much more sympathetic to me, making her vulnerable to my dashing manly charms."

I covered my mouth to stifle my grin and hopefully bury my laugh. "That's brilliant." An overstatement, to be sure. But the guy needed a boost in his confidence to pull this one off.

"Shall we walk arm in arm, making sure she sees us?" He held out his elbow for my hand.

This could be fun, except that we had to end with a fight. "So, what's the plan? How should we argue?"

"Let me remind you, this was your idea."

I risked a glimpse at the young woman. She hadn't seen us yet. With so many others wandering the lobby, how could we get her to notice? "We might need to be dramatic to get her attention."

Spencer nodded then pulled me close. "Let's just agree that it's all for show, nothing to be taken seriously." He turned me to face him, bringing his face near to mine. "Agreed, Polly?"

His voice sounded husky, and I struggled to answer. "Agreed. Nothing we do here should be taken seriously."

Then Spencer kissed me. Thoroughly. I lost myself. Hadn't this been what I'd wanted since I'd seen him? My head screamed at my heart that it was all a charade.

Chaos filled my mind as joy brimmed inside. I pushed away from him, and the dazed expression on his face further confused me.

I didn't know what to think. He'd made sure I agreed that it was all a pretense to gain the receptionist's attention. Did that include his kiss? The very idea sent outrage through me. I'd looked forward to the moment we'd kiss, if ever, as sacred somehow. But now he'd ruined it by using the situation to his benefit, playing me, as it were.

"All right. If you want to play games, then I have this for you." I slapped him full across the face.

He stepped back, stunned. "What was that for?"

My knees shook. How much in our staged argument was real?

"For taking advantage of me." I stomped away, breathless with rage and hurt, my emotions genuine. Once outside, I leaned over the rim wall and watched the lake below, hoping to gain my composure and some sense of decorum. What had just happened back there?

I began my usual overanalyzing. To state that all was done in pretense and then kiss me—did it mean that he didn't really want to? I made my way back inside and into a darkened corner of the lobby where I could watch the scene unfold. Spencer had already begun chatting with the cute blond. The plan had worked.

Then why did I feel so defeated inside? I turned away, unable to watch him with her. This wasn't such a good idea after all.

I couldn't just stand around while he flirted, so I decided to find Emily. Maybe I could simply ask her what her name was. It never hurt to try the usual method. Another stroll outside would do me good, and I could start my search for Emily there. I phoned Mom to invite her along.

She answered on the first ring. "Feel like some fresh air?"

"Oh, Polly, I'm sorry I've been such a bore this entire trip. I just settled down with a good movie. Perhaps you'd like to join me."

My spirits sagged. She'd spent too much time in her room, and I blamed myself. "Maybe next time. Listen, when all this mess is over, why don't you come out to the coast and visit me for a while." *If you're not in prison.* I wanted to kick myself for the unbidden thought.

"I think that would be nice. But I need to get my finances straightened out first. You know, Alec's scam and all that."

I bit my lip to keep from blurting out that she should be more concerned that the rangers believe she was innocent of his murder. "I'm sure everything will work out. In the meantime, how about breakfast with me tomorrow?"

"Sure, I'll call you when I get up."

Though I warned myself against it, I glanced toward the reception desk before heading outside. Spencer and the blond were nowhere in sight. Someone else had taken her place. Now what? He'd better come up with something good.

I strolled outside into the still-bright summer evening, keeping a lookout for Emily. A young couple moseyed past, obviously in love. They reminded me of Rene and Conrad. I'd not seen them all day. Was spending so much time together right before the wedding a good thing? I'd think in Rene's book of superstitions it would be anything but. Hopefully they wouldn't end up fighting and calling the entire thing off. Again.

I was grateful I hadn't run into them or been required to spend an overabundance of time with Rene. How could I investigate then? Add to that, a heavy cloud had moved in and hovered over me now. I wouldn't want to bring her down.

Maybe the events of the last couple of days were finally taking their toll. I considered calling it quits and getting a good night's sleep. But it was only seven. I had to make sure Spencer was not with the other woman. I almost laughed out loud as I moved to the stone rim overlooking the lake. So, things had come to this.

Jealousy.

Hadn't I forced him into her arms? I shook my head at my crazy, wild imaginings—I'd allowed them to go too far, giving my mind too much leeway and imagining suspicious activity where there'd been none. Not only in the case of Spencer and the cute blond, but perhaps I'd presumed too much where Emily and Peter and Hillary were concerned, allowing paranoia to cloud my judgment. I resolved that I'd only focus on hard facts, like the photograph that had led me to question Hillary and, in turn, the information she'd given.

But would it be enough to discover Alec's killer? I sent up a prayer for direction again, feeling that I'd lost whatever internal murder investigation compass I'd possessed.

"There you are." A familiar voice I'd heard that day, but couldn't place, spoke from behind.

Peter stood next to me, also looking over the rim. Immediately his words about pushing someone over the rim came back to me. But what did they mean other than he was somewhat morbid?

I moved away from the edge. "Hi. What are you up to?" Crazy question. But what did you say to a tour guide at the end of the day? "Finished with the tours?"

"Just stopped by to make good on my offer."

I shook my head, my thoughts a blur.

"I offered to give you and your fancy camera a tour of Thomason Island."

Now I remembered. I'd said I would think about it. But I hadn't, and now I couldn't recall if at the time I considered his offer a good or a bad thing. Might Peter's offer be the dreaded fork in the road I feared? Waves of exhaustion tumbled over me, and maybe that added to my depressed state after the staging of a quarrel with Spencer. In any case, I was in no frame of mind to make the right choice. "I'm wondering if this is such a good time. It's getting cold. It'll be dark soon."

"Not for more than a couple of hours. This isn't the sort of tour just anyone can get." He smiled again, this time completely disarming me. "This is a private tour."

An exclusive viewing of Thomason Island tempted me. I might grab scenery not previously photographed, helping me to break into a travel magazine or two. I inclined my head and peered at Peter. Considering that he gave the boat tours, he couldn't have killed Alec, could he? It was all nonsense—wild imaginings again. Still, his information wasn't enough to convince me.

"I can show you some places no other photographers have been."

How did he know? "Why me?"

He leaned in, speaking in low tones so only I could hear. "I've heard rumors that some photographer's been asking questions. I've got some answers." Then he grinned, not unlike Spencer. A tiny part of me thought of getting back at Spencer. After all, he'd not refused to go flirt with Miss Bleached Blond Diva-Wannabe. On that count, I was pathetic.

Of course Peter knew I'd asked questions, because I'd questioned him. If Peter had answers, maybe they would connect with what Hillary had told me somehow. Was this the direction I'd prayed for? Another puzzle piece would go a long way to discovering who'd been in my room and stuffed her in the closet.

"At the island, you say?" I wondered how many others would be there. As long as our tour didn't take me to a room with a closet, I saw no threat.

"If it makes you feel better, we won't be alone. I take a few of the summer volunteers over for some free time every evening."

I looked down at the cone-shaped landmass in the lake then back at him and nodded.

I followed Peter to his truck—a four-wheel drive SUV, not unlike Ranger Jennings's. When Peter helped me up, he took my arm brusquely, which was different than when he'd helped me off the tour boat. When I was secure in his vehicle, his smile faded until it was completely gone.

Quint was back, along with the paranoia.

CHAPTER FOURTEEN

I'd made plenty of mistakes lately and hoped this wasn't another one.

After peeling out of the parking lot, Peter headed to the road encircling the caldera. "I already made my last official boat tour of the day, which includes picking up those I left on the island earlier. The summer volunteers will be waiting. I'd hoped to have you meet me there but didn't have a chance to get you the message. So, here I am." He glanced my way, his grin returning.

"I'm sorry for inconveniencing you."

As he drove, Peter talked about the volunteers, mostly college students who worked for the National Park Service during the summer. This hadn't been a mistake, after all. Hanging around a crowd like that in a relaxed environment was sure to provide clues about the murder, even if it were only hearsay. If nothing else, I could attempt to find out more from Peter. He'd hooked me with bait, tailor-made for me.

"You mentioned you had answers."

With a quick glance and grin, he replied, "In time."

He remained focused on maneuvering the curving road,

which was fine with me, considering the close edge that literally dropped into the lake. The sun would be setting in a couple of hours, and with Thomason Island at the west end of the lake, I wasn't sure I could get very many good photographs. But it was worth a try. As we pulled into the small parking area of Feldman's Shore, dread filled me. In all my deliberations, I hadn't thought of the hike down to the dock.

I'd maneuvered the trail once already today—comparable, they said, to climbing sixty-five flights of stairs. "Isn't there any other way to the island?" I felt like an idiot for asking, but Mom always told me it never hurts to ask.

He pushed his door open and slid halfway out of the truck then turned to me. "'Fraid not."

I sighed and dragged my feet, still feeling the aches and pains from the first trek down. "Are you sure we're going to make it back up before it's dark?"

Peter stopped in his tracks and looked back at me. He squinted, apparently assessing me then frowned. "Maybe you're right. Twice in one day is hard for someone who's not in tip-top shape."

My jaw dropped. "What's that supposed to mean?" He was right, of course. I wasn't in the sort of shape required to compete in a triathlon, which in my estimation was the prerequisite to hiking that trail twice in one day.

"This wasn't a good idea." He started back toward his SUV.

I scratched my head, too tired to make a decision. "I didn't say I didn't want to go. I'm just not sure I can make it." Nor did I want to make the hike at night. One wrong step. . . "Just tell me if we'll be back before dark."

He opened the door for me. "Get in."

I wanted to argue with both Peter and myself. My indecision had cost me the opportunity to listen to college kids potentially discuss the murder. I climbed into the SUV. A vehicle pulled up in the parking lot near the entrance and dropped off a tall man and a short blond woman who quickly exited onto the trail. They reminded me of Spencer and the receptionist. At least if I'd gone with Peter to Thomason Island, I wouldn't have had time to think about them.

On the other hand, maybe I should have stayed at the lodge and monitored the situation between Spencer and the receptionist. "I suppose it's best for me to get back anyway. But wait, how will the volunteers get to the island without you?"

"They can get there without me." Peter drove the vehicle out of the parking lot, peeling out again—an action I considered unusual for a man who looked to be in his midthirties. Maybe it was just a guy thing, and I'd spent too much time with Murphy to know.

Shoving back the regret, I considered how to redeem the situation. "Maybe tomorrow I'll feel better, then you can take me on the private tour. I read there are a couple of trails on the island. I could even explore it myself. I mean, if you don't have time. I could probably find those photographic points on my own, don't you think?"

Peter glanced over at me and held my gaze instead of watching the snakelike road, making me nervous. Finally he returned his attention to his driving. "Sure you could. If you're up to being stuck on the island all day without facilities and with only the food and water you bring with you. There's no guarantee that any of the tourist boats will have room to take you back before the evening pickup. It can be done. Plenty do it."

I pressed back into the vinyl seat. "But you don't think I can, do you?" I thought about my race down the trail, running from an imagined predator. I owned beachfront property. Why hadn't I taken advantage of it and gone for a jog once in a while?

"Look, it's not an insult. Not everyone is cut out for that sort of thing. Imagine being on the island all day, at the end of which you'd have to make the climb up Feldman's Shore Trail again. We caution people to avoid those situations unless they're fully capable and prepared. I misread you earlier today, or I wouldn't have invited you to the island this evening."

He turned onto what looked like a dirt road too small for an SUV. "I'm not sure you could make it tomorrow. You'll probably still be too sore."

I gripped the handle of the door, supporting myself against the bumpy road. "Where are you taking me?"

"I have an idea." He gripped the steering wheel to keep the vehicle from bouncing off the road. "This will work out better for both of us."

I focused on the road ahead. If I needed to make a run for it, all I had to do was follow it back. That, and escape Mr. Triathlete. Otherwise, I had no idea where we were and wished Spencer had known about my traipsing off with the boat tour guide to who knows where. He wouldn't have let me go alone.

Peter pulled to a stop in front of a small building. After he climbed out of the SUV, he stuck his head through the open window, where I remained seated. "You coming?"

I hadn't decided yet. I was alone in the woods with what amounted to a stranger. "What are we doing?"

"If you want to see something beautiful, we're going to hike a trail. Don't worry, it's not too far." He trudged off.

Relieved at his answer, I sensed nothing sinister in his demeanor, and honestly, at this point—and I hated admitting my stupidity—if he'd wanted to harm me, he could have done it. I got out as fast as I could. His legs were longer. I'd have to work hard to keep up. How long would it take to hike to the viewpoint? The hiking trail narrowed so that I couldn't walk next to Peter. I followed like an obedient puppy and tried to ignore more wild imaginings that he'd put me in a bag and throw me into the lake. The forest thickened, making it hard to believe it would ever open up to an observation point.

The trail steepened. Before long, I began breathing hard and sweating, glad there wasn't anyone but Peter to see. A squirrel snickered in a tree somewhere, sounding like laughter. In squirrel-speak, he'd probably told his friends to come watch the show.

I vowed to avoid ever attending a wedding held at a national park again. But Rene was the only serious nature freak I knew personally, so unless she remarried for some reason, this scenario wasn't likely to reoccur. I trudged up the trail, focusing on one step after another. A quick glance ahead stopped me.

A smirk on his face, Peter stood with one hand on his hip, looking at me.

"How. . .much. . .farther?" I could barely manage the question through gasps.

"Just over that rise." He glanced at his watch. "You have time to catch your breath. You may not believe me now, but once we get there, you'll see it's easier than Feldman's Shore Trail." He tossed a bottled water to me. I'd not even noticed he carried it. Some sleuth I was turning out to be.

"Thanks." I took a long, refreshing gulp. "So, why are you helping me find photographic places?"

He looked away and shrugged. His avoidance of the question unnerved me.

"Is this something you do all the time then? Or are you ready to give me those answers?" I took a swipe at tiny flying pests that seemed bent on annoying me.

"We'd better get going." He turned his back on me and started up the trail again.

I fought the urge to run in front of him to demand an answer— like I had that much energy. If I ever decided to journal my life, I'd make sure to delete the part where I acted like an idiot. This time, either I'd let my exhaustion overrule my better judgment, or I was once again being paranoid.

Everyone wasn't a killer. I repeated the words to myself as I trudged forward.

Suddenly Peter's boots came into view. I pulled my gaze up in time to keep from running into him.

The sight I saw past him took away what little breath I had. "It's. . .incredible. You can see for miles. Maybe even a hundred." Hills carpeted in green surrounded a lush valley and huge lake. Farther on, mountain peaks were hazy in the distance, some snowcapped, even in July. To my right, sand dunes occupied part of the national park.

He smiled and held his hand out for me to move past. At once I lifted my camera, taking snapshots until his hand gripped my arm and yanked me backward. I yelped.

He pointed to the ground where I stood. "Be careful. You

don't want to get too close to the edge."

The height made me dizzy. I looked at him, all my ridiculous, paranoid fears dissipating. "Thank you."

If he'd wanted to kill me, that would have been his chance. He could have let me walk right off the cliff's edge, so absorbed was I in taking photographs. And it would have been an accident.

I took a few more snapshots then gave it a rest. Peter had crossed his arms and was staring out into the open space, looking deep in thought.

He turned his pensive gaze on me. "The sun will be dropping behind those peaks soon. The most beautiful sight you'll ever see. Then we'll have to hurry down the trail. It grows dark fast in the canopy."

"I understand. This is such a beautiful place; why isn't it open to the public?"

"Mostly time, manpower, and money to make it safe. I like that there are places still off-limits to the public." He stared beyond me, seemingly engrossed in the scenery.

In his silence, I took more pictures.

"How's Mrs. Jennings? Were you able to learn anything about the murder from her?"

I lowered my camera, his words garbled in my mind. I thought he had answers. These were questions. And what with a killer still out there and what had happened to Hillary, it wasn't a question I wanted to hear from Peter right now. He'd set me back on alarm. What exactly did he know about my conversation with Hillary?

It took me a full fifteen seconds to respond. "Um. . .what makes you ask?"

"I want to know what Hillary—I mean, Mrs. Jennings—told

you about the murder. Why shouldn't I ask?"

"But how did you know I talked to her?"

Now I saw why he'd taken a special interest in me. He'd dangled answers to get me up here. But he was the one who wanted answers. Without a gift for perceiving danger, I was out of my depth when it came to sleuthing.

"I had a break this afternoon and came back to the lodge, hoping to ask you to meet me at the trailhead later. Then I learned that Mrs. Jennings had been hurt and went to see her. You were there ahead of me. I didn't have time to wait around."

"And you think I was asking her about the murder?"

He glared at me. "Ms. Perkins. I'm not a moron."

Idiot! I'd called myself that a lot lately.

Here I stood on a precipice with a magnificent view because of its height, and no one knew where I was. No one would ever find me. I moved toward the wooded area, away from him. This was it. I was about to experience DEFCON 1, defined as an imminent attack from a foreign power. The look Peter was giving me definitely came across as foreign.

My teeth chattered uncontrollably. Wishing my camera still worked as therapy, I backed into a large boulder, cornered like a small rat terrier with Peter as the pit bull. A glance to my left revealed the trail. He already knew I wasn't in great shape.

When he took a step toward me, I pressed against the boulder in a frozen panic.

Lord, please help me.

"Relax, Ms. Perkins. You look like you might die of a heart attack. Like you think I'm the killer. I'm not."

"How do I know that?"

"Because you'd be dead already if I was."

Of course. I'd said the same thing to myself.

Was it considered rational to believe someone who might be a killer when they told you they weren't? There was only one way for me to be sure.

Steeling my nerves, I fumbled my camera into position. "Can I take your picture?" Would he remember I'd asked the same of him on the boat?

"Huh?" He scratched his head. "Oh yeah, no problem. Honestly, it surprised me that you came here with me alone. But I figured that you knew I wasn't the killer or you never would have done it." He rubbed his hand over his jaw. "I suppose I read you wrong on that, too. I overestimated you."

His words both calmed my nerves and irritated me at the same time. "Now, wait just a minute."

He stuck his hands out, palms down. "No need to be offended. I brought you up here where we could speak in private. But I also wanted you to see the sunset. It's almost on us. Why don't you answer my question, then you can take more pictures if you like, and afterward we can make our way down the trail before it's completely dark."

The sigh that came from me sounded like a tire deflating— it was that long. His question about Hillary made me think he knew something about the murder himself. But I wouldn't say that to him. This time, I'd let him *under*estimate me.

"I'll answer your question if you'll answer one of mine first." It sounded like we were competing sleuths. Could Peter be conducting his own investigation?

"It depends on the question. Go for it."

"Do you think Alec deserved to die?" Hearing myself state the question a second time to Peter, I realized it was a trick question of sorts. Like when I asked Spencer if he saw the cute blond at the reception desk. Fortunately for him, he'd answered wisely.

He, like any man, knew that even if he chose his words very carefully, his answer could be taken wrong. I prayed I wouldn't misconstrue Peter's answer.

"I think Alec Gordon had plenty of enemies."

"I already know that."

"Have you considered Chief Ranger Jennings?"

CHAPTER FIFTEEN

Back at the lodge, I was too wired to go to bed even though I'd had an exhausting day. The mountain air had chilled considerably with nightfall, yet I stood outside against the stone-protected lake rim, allowing the wind to thrash my hair against my face—a punishment of sorts for my commonsense deficiency. At least with a vitamin deficiency you might only end up with rickets, but in a murder investigation my ailment could kill me.

Have you considered Chief Ranger Jennings? Peter's words had left me tongue-tied. Ranger Jennings as the murderer had never entered my mind. No wonder Peter took me to a remote location. He didn't want to risk being overheard accusing a ranger, the law enforcement of national parks.

More than ever, I needed to talk to Spencer. He'd not considered the ranger either, or else he'd have brought it up when I told him about Hillary's affair. Maybe, like I had, he assumed the ranger wasn't aware his wife was cheating.

Before I found him, though, I had to make sure I reined in my emotions. I shoved aside any jealous thoughts of Spencer with the receptionist and instead hoped that he'd learned something.

Part of me still burned with his untimely kiss, though I'd had a chance to cool off. After reexamining what happened, I could come to no other conclusion—I'd overreacted. When facing matters of the heart, acting with an ounce of brain was never easy.

The bottom line: I resolved never to let my guard down again. Yeah, right.

"There you are." Arms grabbed me and pulled me into a warm embrace from behind. "I've been worried about you." Spencer whispered against my ear, his breath warm.

Oh, how I wanted to savor his embrace and forget about his staged kiss. Pulling free, I tried to appear nonchalant. "So, how did it go with what's-her-name?" I cringed at the jealous-sounding words.

"Aren't you cold out here?" He turned me to look at him, his face far too close.

It reminded me of the incident only a few hours before. "I was just about to go in."

"Good, I could use a cup of hot. . .er, cocoa."

I couldn't help but smile. "Are you trying to become more American? Choosing hot cocoa over your tea?"

"Yes, if that would please you." He opened the door for me, and I stepped into the warmth of the lodge, the walls reflecting shadows created by the giant fire.

He led the way to a group of tables in the corner of the Terrace Café, the inside part where people shared a late-evening drink.

After pulling my chair out, he sat across from me. "What's wrong, Polly? You don't look happy to see me."

A young woman came and took our drink orders. "It's been a

very long day. I'd like to hear if you discovered anything."

He seemed pleased enough to see me, so maybe he hadn't enjoyed his time with the receptionist too much. "Ah, yes. Well first, let me congratulate you on what a fine actress you are. Spot on, Polly." He leaned against the chair back and grinned.

I supposed he'd poured that same charm on the receptionist. "What are you talking about?"

"Why, the slap, of course. You slapped me across the face. That was brilliant. Very convincing."

The hot chocolate arrived. Spencer sipped his slowly, as did I while I considered his comment. The drink warmed my insides, making me realize I had become chilled and hadn't even noticed. When I looked up, he was studying me.

"Feeling better?"

I smiled. "Yes, thanks."

His expression turned serious again. "Can I ask you something?"

"What's stopping you?"

He set down his cup. "Yes, well, see. From the vibes I'm getting from you, I'm wondering if perhaps the slap was real." He inclined his head slightly but kept eye contact, as though gauging my response.

Avoiding his gaze, I toyed with my hot chocolate, stirring it for a couple of seconds then lifted it to my mouth and sipped. If I told him the slap was real, he'd know how I felt about his kiss—that I'd been hurt he'd used something that should have been a special moment, our first kiss in years. Nothing inherently wrong with that, except I wasn't ready to reveal how I felt about him. How could I be when I wasn't ready to admit my feelings to myself?

I felt that slight brimming of moisture in my eyes that I loathed. It occurred at the most inopportune moments, and this was an inopportune moment.

Fighting the tears, I took another swig of the hot liquid. "You said nothing was to be taken seriously. Sounds like I might have offended you with that. Sorry."

"No problem. We accomplished what we needed to. But I'd like to know where you've been all evening."

"What do you mean? Haven't you been with the receptionist?"

"Ah, no. I spent a few minutes talking to her, maybe thirty, tops. I tried to find you. You scare me when you disappear like that, Polly." With a pained expression he glanced away then back at me, his eyes penetrating. "Please. . .no more."

Guilt rushed through me. He wouldn't be happy about what I had to tell him next. I spent the next few minutes watching him work his jaw while I explained about jaunting off with Peter. His eyes seemed full of pain.

He waited until I was done before he spoke. "Don't ever do that again."

I froze. A knot grew in my throat, making it painful to swallow. Was the controlling Spencer showing himself now?

He leaned back and tugged on his collar. "That didn't come out right. Polly, please, do *not* put yourself in that position again."

With his contrite clarification, did I dare contemplate what appeared to be his deep concern for me? "No, you're right. It all happened so fast. I wasn't prepared. But all the same, I know a few more things." For all of my trying to position myself to pose questions about the murder, Peter had been the one to do it first.

"What? That you should check into Chief Ranger Jennings as

the killer? Why doesn't this Peter do it himself? Polly, I don't like it one bit. Maybe this guy is trying to turn our attention away from him, point the finger elsewhere."

"That's just what Ranger Jennings thought about me when I brought up Hillary. I know the very idea seems crazy. But I hadn't even considered him." Here I was concerned that Hillary Jennings confess her affair to her husband. She seemed convinced that he wasn't aware of it, but what if he'd known all along? "Spencer, if he knows about the affair, then he had motivation to murder Alec Gordon."

"Yes, well, that goes without saying. But are you considering the implications here?" Spencer looked around. Only one other couple was left, sitting at a table at the far corner. "Any law-enforcement official who would commit a murder would be more than eager to pin it on someone else."

"Which means I need to figure things out—and fast."

Spencer frowned. "I'd like to hear you use the word 'we' from now on. *We* need to find out who killed Alec, whether it was Ranger Jennings or someone else. Though to tell you the truth, I'd rather turn everything we know over to the authorities."

"Well, we can't exactly do that now if Chief Ranger Jennings is the murderer, can we?"

"At some point, we'll have to. But I agree that it's imperative we find the evidence we need to point to him, if he is the murderer, before he can pin the murder on someone else. A word of caution, Polly—we don't know that it's him."

"You're right. We don't. Now, why don't you tell me what you found out?"

"You're going to find it interesting as well."

"Go on." One glance told me we were the only ones left in the café.

"Two things, actually. Your friend Emily? She's registered as Raquel Kendall. More importantly, she requested a safe-deposit box to keep valuables."

I drew in a sharp breath. "Now that's something. There are pieces to the same puzzle here, but I'm not sure how they fit. Anything else?"

"The receptionist made a comment that I didn't understand before, but now I think I'm getting it. She said she wouldn't be surprised if Ranger Jennings turned a blind eye to whoever murdered Alec Gordon. That he was probably glad the man was gone."

"Now what a strange thing to say." I'd finished my hot chocolate and tipped the cup back and forth, my nerves on edge.

"Sounds like other people knew about their affair. Most likely even Ranger Jennings." Spencer arched his brow. "Another thought occurs to me. Anyone who knew of the affair could easily use that information to their advantage, by say, setting things up to look like Hillary killed him."

"Or anyone else for that matter. That makes this sleuthing more difficult." I yawned widely then slapped my hand over my mouth. "Oh, I'm so sorry, Spencer."

"You should get some rest. Clearing that brilliant mind of yours will help to sort things out. Just. . .be careful."

"Sure. You, too. You did a great job retrieving information from her. Mind if I ask how you did it?" I was scared to hear the answer but had to know.

"Funny thing, that."

"Yes, well, I'm waiting."

He grinned. "She was intrigued with my accent, as you thought. Is studying to become a translator. Wants to be an international traveler. I thought she'd hit things off great with my sister, so I invited her up to the castle."

"You didn't." He'd invited me as well. Had he really invited her to his parents' estate to meet his sister? "Well, I think you're right. I need to get to bed."

"Let me escort you."

"No, it's all right."

"I insist."

I was too tired to argue. We strolled through the lobby. Once inside an elevator, Spencer pushed the second-floor button. I leaned back against the wall, a myriad of thoughts scrambling through my mind. How did Spencer really feel about me? Had the housekeeper been set up for the murder of a man who had many enemies? Had Mom enjoyed her movie? Was she still awake? Where in the world did Rene and Conrad go?

The door opened, and I stepped out, wishing Spencer a good night. He followed me out into the corridor. I pretended that I didn't care whether or not he was there—it seemed the only way to maintain control. After finding my card key, I readied to shove it into the slot.

Spencer stopped me. "Polly. . ."

As I looked into his face, I remembered my vow to guard myself. "Yes, well, it's getting late. Thank you for escorting me to my room. I'm sure you don't need to go in and check everything." I giggled, nervous at Spencer's nearness.

He rubbed my arms. "About the little show we put on. I know

I said not to take it seriously. But. . .I meant the kiss."

His soft words stole my breath. I shook my head to break the spell and squinted at him. "Um. . .it sounded like you just said you meant the kiss." My emotions swung between anger and pure joy. The hall was so quiet that my swallow seemed to echo down the corridor.

"Yes. That's what I said." Spencer's voice had gone husky again. He leaned in close and waited, as though he needed my permission this time. "I just wanted you to know that the kiss was real for me. That's why it occurred to me that your slap might also have been real."

"I—I thought you'd kissed me without being serious, that you were toying with me." His face was so close I could feel his breath on my cheeks. I closed my eyes.

"So you won't slap me if I kiss you again?"

Without waiting for my reply, his lips pressed against mine, wrapping me with his strong emotion, with tenderness, with everything I'd dreamed of and hoped for.

Except this time, I knew it was real.

I wanted to melt into him. But this wasn't the kind of passion one unbridled without the proper vows in place. When finally I stood inside my room, my back against the door, I wondered how I got there. I happened to remember Spencer's urgent reminder to bolt the door once inside. From there I flipped on the rest of the lights.

My computer lay on the floor, smashed to bits, along with another expensive camera I'd brought.

CHAPTER ⛩ SIXTEEN

At three in the morning, I was unable to sleep and stared at the darkness as I lay in bed, considering the events of the last few hours. To say that I'd had a bad night was an understatement. After getting over the initial shock that someone had destroyed my equipment, I debated whether to call security. Would calling mean I'd face Ranger Jennings in the middle of the night?

Ultimately I'd called the lodge operator, who directed me to security, which they'd increased since the murder. I figured I might need to have it on record that I'd returned to my room to find my equipment destroyed, in case Ranger Jennings decided to point the finger at me.

After the security guard had taken my statement, he assured me that bolting the door would be enough to keep me safe. I wondered about the rest of the time, when I wasn't in my room. Apparently people were free to come and go in lodge rooms despite the locks.

I decided against calling Spencer. He would worry about me, and there was nothing he could do anyway. I touched my lips, remembering his kiss—the real deal this time. I was still scared to death that he was setting me up for a big fall. But I couldn't blame him because—who was I kidding?—I was allowing it to happen.

The puzzle pieces of Alec's murder awaited my attention, for which I was grateful. All the pieces seemed to turn colors that could belong to the same picture. But how did they fit together?

Someone knocked on my door, sending a shock of nervous fear through me. What now?

My heart pounded against my chest like it wanted out as I tiptoed to the door and looked through the peephole. "Mom!"

Deadbolts, I discovered, weren't designed to be opened by the distressed. Once my fumbling brought success, Mom traipsed into my room, clothed only in her nightgown and robe. She was barefoot.

"What's going on? Why are you up in the middle of the night?" I asked.

Without responding, she walked over to the closet and opened the door, looked inside, then shut it. Then she moved to the television and turned it on.

I went to where she sat on the bed and waved my hand in front of her face. Her eyes stared straight ahead. "I don't believe this. You're sleepwalking?"

I'd heard that sleepwalkers weren't supposed to be awakened, but what did one do in this situation? What could possibly happen? As I considered my options, I continued to watch her.

The idea that she was sleepwalking and had gone to the closet and looked inside disturbed me. Utterly. I'd heard of sleep driving, sleep cooking. . .but what about sleep killing? What if she actually *had* killed Alec Gordon?

I hurried to the bathroom to grab a glass of water, uncertain whether I should have her drink it or just toss it in her face.

When I came out, she'd turned the television off and was standing at my desk, staring blankly at the remnants of my computer and camera.

"Mom, how about a drink of water?" I thrust it in her face, hoping for a response. When none came, I pressed it against her lips.

Ignoring me, she turned and headed for the door. Where would she go? Another unwelcome and horrible thought accosted me. Would she lead me to the murder weapon? As I watched her exit, I forced the morbid imaginings from my mind. She left the door open wide behind her. I stared after her, grabbing the hoodie off the end of my bed. I'd have to guide her back to her room. Before the door shut, I remembered the key and grabbed it.

Mom never understood why I didn't wear a nightgown like her. Tonight proved there was one good thing about wearing sweats and a T-shirt to bed—I was always ready for encounters of the strange kind, especially those occurring in the middle of the night.

Once out the door, I saw Mom sauntering down the hall toward the elevators. "Mom!" I hissed in my loudest whisper, hoping I wouldn't disturb other sleepers.

She moved like she would pass the elevators. I put my hands on her shoulders and gently guided her toward them. They opened as soon as I pushed the button, a first to be sure. Mom walked right in. She waited with me as the box moved to her floor. If I thought the elevators had moved slowly before, they seemed to take an eternity now. I used the time to talk to Mom. Maybe waking her would have been a better idea.

I wondered about my prayers for direction. "Lord, did I forget to pray for direction in the last thirty minutes? If so, I could use some help here."

The elevator dinged—normally a pleasant sound in the middle of the day. In the dead of night, it was the town bell ringing to call everyone to the church for the impending town meeting or, instead, to warn of a coming disaster and take cover. The last thing I needed was to draw attention to this eccentric activity in the middle of the night during a murder investigation.

Without any nudging, Mom walked straight to her door.

The key! Would she have her key with her? Did sleepwalkers have the frame of mind to think of such things?

Mom pulled something from her pocket. I sagged against the wall, relieved that I wouldn't have to drag her back to my room. She stuck it into the thin slot, but it wouldn't trip the lock. On closer examination I saw that it wasn't the card key at all.

"Mom, what is that?" I took it from her hands. It was a small memory card—the sort of thing that would fit into a camera. My camera. Mom still used the old 35mm film. "Where did you get this?"

I heaved a sigh, hoping she'd come willingly with me back to my room, which on second thought was for the best. In fact, I sent up a "thank You" for the Lord's guidance.

Praying the entire way, I hoped we wouldn't run into anyone. I would have to do some explaining if we were questioned, and this seemed a bizarre story to add to an already long list of bizarre stories. We turned the corner into the corridor where my room was. I heard the door open at the end of the hall and caught a glimpse of someone as they exited the hallway. Whoever it was glanced back, but it was too quick and dark for me to see a face. I noticed a rag hanging from a back pocket.

We sauntered in slow sleepwalker fashion down the length of the hallway back to my room. Once inside, Mom lay down without a fuss on the double bed that I hadn't used, snuggling up to an extra pillow. I shut off all the lights except for a small one next to the chair in the corner, where I curled my legs under me to watch Mom.

I grabbed my Nikon—thankfully it was still intact—and traded out the memory card with the one Mom had tried to open her door with. As I suspected, it was one of mine, containing some older photographs. When had she taken this card? I recalled she was standing next to the desk when I'd come out of the bathroom with the water.

I shook my head, feeling perplexed—just one more emotion to add to my overloaded circuits. If only I were a computer, I could expand my brainpower and memory.

But that probably wouldn't be an option, even in the next century. So I processed one thought at a time. With Mom popping sleeping pills during the day and night, there was no way of knowing what she'd been up to. That is, if she made sleepwalking any sort of habit. Add to that, her peek in my closet. I rubbed my arms to coax away the goose bumps.

Mom was no murderer. Could someone commit that sort of crime without knowing it? Had she been the one to smash my computer and camera and take the memory card because her alter mind or personality or ego—I knew nothing of psychobabble— thought it held incriminating pictures of her committing the murder? I grabbed the hair on both sides of my head, wanting to pull hard and scream.

This time I allowed the tears to slide freely down my cheeks. "Oh, Mom." The words came out in a choked whisper. After I'd spent the tears, one other question demanded attention.

What was George Hamilton doing in my hallway in the middle of the night?

—

"Polly!"

At hearing my name, my eyes popped open. Mom's face was big in my field of vision. I cried out and jerked away from her. Pain shot through my legs and neck. I'd fallen asleep scrunched in the chair.

"Ow! Mom, what are you. . ." Then I remembered. One glance at the clock and I panicked. "Ten thirty! Mom, we've overslept." I disentangled myself from the ill-suited bed.

"Why am I in your room?" Confusion and fear blazed across her face.

"You were sleepwalking last night. You came to my room." I saved the part about her going to her room with my memory card as a key for another conversation.

Her mouth sagged open as though absorbing what I'd said took too much energy for her to operate both her mind and mouth. Eventually the power came back on. "I can't believe that."

"Well, it's got to be those new sleeping pills. You said you feel tired all the time. Now we know why."

"We do?"

"Yes, Mother." I put strong emphasis on calling her "Mother"—something I rarely did—to get her attention, like when mothers call their children by their full name. She needed to know I meant business. "You haven't been sleeping at all. You've been doing other things." I cleared my throat. "Apparently."

"But it's crazy that I would walk to your room without waking up."

"I can't argue with you there. I'm getting dressed, then we're going to move you in with me. And we're getting rid of those sleeping pills, do you understand me?"

"But how am I going to make it—"

"I'm brooking no argument on this. Sleepwalking like you were last night, that could be dangerous."

Mom slumped onto the edge of the bed and bit her nail. I hadn't seen her do that before, but perhaps she did it in lieu of a cigarette, given her renewed interest in smoking. I hoped she would continue to bite her nails if it meant she wouldn't smoke. I wasn't sure how I could tolerate it in my room.

"Polly." She gasped my name like she'd just watched me die. "You don't think—"

"Stop. Don't even go there. You're not a murderer, even in your sleep." *Please, no, God.*

"Well, that does explain one thing."

I wasn't sure I wanted to know.

"All those Jesus, Mary, and Joseph dolls I purchased from that infomercial."

Any other time, that news would have made me laugh, especially if it weren't so scary that one little pill could put a person out of control of their faculties. But considering a murder had been committed and Mom had said she wanted to kill the guy, the church bell of alarm clanged in my head.

I phoned the concierge to tell them we planned to move into one room. Then I looked at Mom in her nightgown and robe. "You'll have to wear something of mine unless you want to go down like that to get your key. They won't give me the key to your room."

"Oh all right. Mind if I shower first?"

"Go right ahead. But please hurry." I had the distinct feeling that the answer to Alec's murder was within my grasp, hidden somewhere in the few clues we'd gathered. If I put the pieces on the table, maybe I could fit them together.

The phone rang. Well, I knew it wasn't Mom. Thoughts of Spencer made my stomach flutter inside. I wondered why he'd waited so late to call. "Hello?"

"Polly. This is Bridget."

Getting a call from my assistant at my portrait studio was the last thing I expected. "Bridget. Hi, how are you?" I tried to keep the frustration and impatience from my voice. After all, I had left her in charge of my business.

"Oh, I'm fine. It's that dog of yours that's the problem."

Murphy. "Surely you can tolerate him for a few more days. If not, just put him with boarding. He'll live." I cringed as I said those hateful words, but I couldn't take on another problem. Not today.

"You don't understand," she said.

"Well, then, why don't you explain?" This was Bridget's way of talking, and at any other time, I would be amused.

"He's gone. I haven't seen him since yesterday."

Oh no. "Are you serious?"

"Of course. I just thought you should know."

"Um. . .have you looked for him?" I wished I could rush home.

I didn't feel I could trust anyone else to make a thorough search for him.

"Of course I have."

"Where? Tell me where you've looked. I'm sorry, Bridget, I just need for you to find him. He's my companion, ya know?" I thought of all the evenings I'd spent, watching movies and sharing popcorn with Murphy.

"Trust me, I've looked everywhere."

I rubbed my temple. Where could he be? "I can't come back until the wedding is over. Call me if you find him, okay?" I'd almost mentioned the murder investigation, but I didn't feel like explaining that to Bridget, who would bug me until I spilled all the details.

After I hung up, Mom came out of the bathroom after her quick shower. Despite oversleeping, I took my turn—and my time—trying to wash away the exhaustion of the last few days and the news of Murphy's disappearance.

"Lord, You promise never to give us more than we can handle. I'm absolutely positive that I can't handle one more thing. My cup runneth over with all manner of bad things. In fact, it's teetering on the edge of a table. One more thing and I'm sure it'll tip and fall to the floor, dashed to smithereens."

After Brandon disappeared, I'd tried to learn how to give my burdens to the Lord. I realized that I had forgotten to do that this weekend. My problems were more than the loss of Brandon. I did what I could to empty my heart to God.

Once I finished showering, I wiped at the steamy mirror then toweled my hair dry. I felt drained but in a good way—I was completely empty of the burdensome feelings.

But I wondered if that meant I needed to be ready for more. . . .
Mom knocked on the door. *Here we go again.*

"Polly, you in there?"

"Where else would I be?" Surely she didn't think I'd gone down the drain.

"It's Bridget. She wants to talk to you."

I hadn't meant the sarcastic tone before and made sure to correct it. "Okay, give me a sec." Pulling sweats over my still damp body proved to be a challenge. Steam joined me as I exited the bathroom.

I grabbed the phone. "Bridget, what's the news?"

"I found him! Polly, I found him."

I closed my eyes, allowing myself complete peace with the news. "Where was he?"

"The little dickens. You're not going to believe this. He was in the prop room in a box of costumes. You know the ones you keep for special photo shoots."

"Oh, I'm so glad! You have no idea."

"He's so cute. I took some pictures. I'll e-mail them to you. He'd somehow managed to come out of the box with a hat on his head, almost like that TV dog—"

"Wishbone." While keeping Murphy for Mom, I learned quickly enough that the breed was nothing at all like the television version of the dog. "Thanks, Bridget, for holding down the fort. Just a couple more days, okay?"

"Sure thing, Polly."

I hung up and sat on the bed, feeling exuberant as I pictured Murphy adorned in a disguise. That's when two pieces of the who-killed-Alec-Gordon puzzle in my head slid together.

CHAPTER SEVENTEEN

The fact that Murphy helped me decipher a clue to Alec's murder completely debunked my earlier theory about him causing everything to go wrong. I almost regretted that he'd been named Murphy.

Given Mom's propensity to wear the theme-of-the-day clothing, I developed an eye for particular everyday fashion outrages. And Emily was an eyesore. Her dark look had drawn attention away from the disparity in her attire—a costume I now believed was a disguise.

"Okay, Mom, something's come up. I'm going to need you to tag along with me today."

"What? You know I can't do that. You're young and energetic. Me? I haven't slept much, remember?"

I quirked a brow. That was a hard call. On the one hand, she'd been asleep while traipsing around the lodge. On the other hand, her body hadn't gotten any rest.

"Which is exactly why you can either tag along or hand over those sleeping pills. You are not to take another one. That's the only way I'll agree for you to be alone."

Mom huffed and paced. "I don't know. I think I might be addicted. You better let me keep them for now."

"There's always that possibility. Tell you what. Why don't you at least try to come with me for a while? You've been cooped up too long as it is."

"But that's because I haven't felt well."

"And exactly why you need to get out and get some fresh air. That will help you feel better."

"All right, but first I need to get into something that matches."

"Good, and then we'll pack your things so you can move in with me."

Mom frowned, but she didn't argue. She probably knew it was for the best, too, considering the scary possibility that she'd done something heinous like commit murder.

After Mom retrieved another key from the registration desk, I escorted her to her room. She turned over her sleeping pills. I promised we'd address addiction problems later, and she promised to dress and pack her things. I'd come back for her within the hour.

I had to find Spencer to discuss what I'd worked out regarding Emily. Reasons why he hadn't called this morning worked their way into my heart like a painful sliver. After kissing me, had he decided we were going too fast? That he still wasn't ready to commit?

I found him all right, sitting at a table with the blond receptionist. Fury almost overshadowed my hurt. I reminded myself of his kiss—that I believed it genuine.

Spencer saw me as I strolled up to the table. "Polly!" He stood, grabbing his chair before it toppled over. "This is Amber. You remember her, don't you?"

I nodded and smiled, afraid to say anything.

Her smile produced a brilliant white set of perfectly straight teeth. "Number 205. Well, I'd better get going. It's almost time for my shift." She nodded at me and left.

"Have a seat. I'd hoped to see you earlier this morning. But I hope you got some rest." Spencer pulled out a chair for me.

If only he knew the sort of night I'd had. "You could have called."

"I kept you up late last night. You looked exhausted, so I didn't want to disturb you."

I toyed with the unused fork. "What's-her-name didn't eat with you?"

"She saw me and sat down to chat for a minute." Spencer reached across the table and grabbed my hand, stopping the clinking noise I was making with the fork against the plate. "Don't worry. I'm not interested in her in the least."

A waiter approached and asked what I'd like for breakfast. "Juice, please."

Rubbing his chin, Spencer gave me a thoughtful look. "You're not hungry?"

Considering I'd tucked Mom in her room to pack, I couldn't eat without her, could I? "Well, maybe just a slice of toast. You haven't heard about my night yet." The waiter promptly returned with juice and toast. I explained everything that had happened around crunching on the toast and drinking two glasses of juice. "So, after I pictured Murphy in a disguise, that's when I realized that Emily—"

"Raquel," Spencer corrected.

"Whatever. I can't think of her as anyone else. Now if you'll allow me to get back to my story."

"As you wish."

"That's when I realized that every time I'd seen her, she was completely decked out in her scary dark clothes, but she wore earrings that didn't match and shoes she wasn't used to walking in. I'm talking emerald-cut diamonds. I suspect she's not who she wants us to think she is."

"Hmm. You may be onto something there."

"I know I am. She's wearing expensive jewelry, and she has a safe-deposit box, so she must have more. George said Alec took something that fell out of Emily's bag, and Hillary said Alec had shown her a large diamond ring that she claims is gone. So now all we need is to find Emily."

"Well, I've got her room number if that helps."

"You do? How'd you'd get it and why?"

"I needed to make haste while I had Amber's ear. Actually, the girl has a photographic memory, and she talks about people by their room numbers, not their names. She called Raquel. . . er. . .Emily, as you call her, Room 422."

"You're kidding." I set my glass of orange juice down. "So that explains her reference to my room number."

"Yes. I've suggested she avoid that; otherwise, she won't last much longer at this job." He leaned forward on his elbows. "Let me ask you something. Will you agree to go to the authorities as soon as we have what we need?"

"Yes. But I want to know who the killer is so there's no doubt, no bungling, no finger-pointing. If you-know-who"— I glanced around to make sure no one was listening, —"committed the murder, I don't want him to put someone else away." As things stood right now, Ranger Jennings could lay the guilt on his wife, Hillary—which I doubted he would do—Mom, or maybe Emily, who was hiding something. I needed to find out more about her.

As for me, I wasn't sure the authorities had lost interest in me yet, but I wondered why Ranger Jennings hadn't talked to me about finding his wife in my closet. With so much else going on, however, there wasn't much point in worrying about that until it happened.

After we paid the bill at the café, we headed to Emily's room, hoping she hadn't already checked out or left for the day. The police could have finished questioning her, giving her permission to leave. As we approached her room, a series of thuds issued from inside, then the door opened. Emily worked to keep it that way with her foot, wrestling with two bags over her shoulders, a suitcase, and a garment bag on wheels.

Her eyes grew wide when she saw us. "What do you want?"

I looked at Spencer. This wouldn't be easy. "Um. . .we need to talk to you."

"I have nothing to say." She shut the door behind her. "Now, get out of my way."

How was I going to keep her from leaving without causing a scene? Might as well get to the point. "I think you killed Alec Gordon."

She pushed past me. "You're crazy, lady."

"All I'm asking is for a few minutes of your time. Or I'll call the rangers right now."

"If you thought I'd killed him and could prove it, you would have already told them." She kept walking.

"I know you're hiding from someone."

She dropped her bags and turned to face me, her gaze darting up and down the hall. "Oh, all right. Let's go back into my room. But I can't talk long."

Strange that calling her a murderer hadn't caused her any distress, but my knowing that she was in hiding had.

Once Emily allowed Spencer and me into her room, things grew more awkward. What would I ask next?

"Look, you got me, all right? I'm trying to escape my husband." She tugged at her hair, removing her long, black mane—a wig—and revealing shoulder-length, ash-blond hair. "I think he's onto me and might be here any minute. So, just tell me what you want. Is it money?"

We needed more time. I looked at Spencer and got his nod of approval. "I don't want your money. Why don't we go to my room? That way you'll be safely hidden, and we'll have more time to talk."

She rolled her head back and looked at the ceiling like an impatient teenager. "This has already taken too long, so let's hurry."

With Emily's wig back in place, Spencer grabbed her bags. We headed to the elevators and waited. Emily chewed on her lip and stared at the floor, exuding disquiet. The elevator dinged—in warning, it seemed—a sign I was suffering from empathetic worry.

We made our way to my room two floors down without running into any trouble—Ranger Jennings, Emily's husband, Mom. . . .

By the time he entered my room, Spencer was nearly breathless.

He shed Emily's luggage and marched straight to the small desk where my computer sat, smashed to pieces.

"Polly." His shoulders sagged. "I had no idea it was this bad. I'm so sorry. Seeing this must have given you a fright." He glanced over at me. "Why didn't you call me?"

The dejected look in his eyes made me wish I had. Shaking my head, I gave him a warning frown and mouthed, "Not now."

Emily seemed not to notice our exchange as she tugged the wig off again then pulled the studs from her nose, lips, and ears to reveal they were all fakes. "The tattoos are temporary. Satisfied?"

"You left the good ones, though."

"What?" Her brows dipped. Understanding dawned and her lips curved slightly, the closest thing to a smile I'd seen on her. She touched the emerald-cut diamonds in her lobes. "These? Yeah, well. I forget to take them out; because I've worn them so long."

I hesitated, considering the best way to proceed. When she squinted at me and tossed a nervous glance at Spencer, it occurred to me that we hadn't introduced ourselves. After explaining who we were, I posed the question burning in my mind since we left Emily's room. "Why are you running from your husband?"

She swallowed and looked from Spencer to me. "He's abusive. I'm afraid for my life." A mixture of fear and sorrow swam in her eyes. "He's wealthy—all drug-related and connected."

Which explained the expensive jewels. "That's why you didn't want me to post any photographs of you, in case he or someone he knew saw them."

"I need to disappear from the face of the earth."

One glance at Spencer told me he believed her, his face ragged with emotion. "So why did you think Caldera National Park would be a safe hiding place?" he asked.

She rubbed her hands together as she paced. "I flirted with someone in a chat room. He seemed so understanding and filled my desperate need to talk to someone—anyone." She stopped pacing and searched Spencer's gaze. Looking for sympathy? I couldn't help but notice she hadn't glanced at me. I didn't like it one bit. Why was she telling us this? She tore her eyes from Spencer's and began pacing again.

"When I decided to escape my husband, to run away and hide, I didn't know where to go. But I remembered the guy I chatted with telling me about coming to this national park. I couldn't imagine a better place to hide. My husband would never look for me here in a rustic lodge in the middle of nowhere. Believe me, I'm not into outdoorsy stuff. But I had to be in order to hide. To be safe. At least for a while." Emily sounded as though she would cry, but she didn't. Her husband had probably toughened her up.

I eyed Spencer, wondering where this information would lead us, if anywhere. Would she say more, connecting herself to Alec? When she sat on the bed and shivered, I decided not to press her. She looked liked someone who'd kept her personal-space bubble so small it deprived her of oxygen. She was desperate for air. For love. Her bubble was ready to burst.

She looked at me. "There's more."

I released the breath I'd held in hopes there would be.

"I didn't know the man who helped me when my luggage spilled on the sidewalk. I brought all the jewelry that my husband had given me over the years in case I needed to sell it for money.

He'd made sure I had nothing to my name, so the jewelry was all I had."

Her sorrow gripped me. Tears slid down her face. What must it be like to be married to a man like that?

"When I got to the lodge, I planned to put the jewelry in a safe-deposit box, including my ring, which I would never wear again. Only I couldn't find it. I suspected that the man who helped me with my luggage had taken it. I kept looking for him, asking around. When I finally saw him, I followed him to his room to confront him, but I lost my nerve. I wanted to remain calm so I would have the upper hand. I left to come back later. When I did. . ." Her voice cracked. "I knocked on the door and it swung open. He wasn't in his room, so I took the liberty of rummaging through his things to find my ring. It belonged to me, after all. I couldn't find it, so I looked in the closet. That's where I found him on the floor. Unconscious or dead, I don't know." Tears flooded her face. "I searched his pocket and found my ring. I took what was mine. But I didn't kill him."

She looked at Spencer, pleading. "You've got to believe me."

Was it some sort of can-I-get-more-sympathy-from-the-man-with-my-pouting-eyes that made her appeal to him rather than me? I stood directly in front of her.

Spencer appeared to be mesmerized by either her or the story. He shook his head and moved from the wall where he'd been leaning. "Emily. . .Raquel."

"Emily?" She looked at me. "That's the same name you called me before. Why do you keep calling me that?"

"Oh, just that, well, when I first saw you in the restroom at the restaurant, you reminded me of Emily the Strange, with your black cats and skulls. You know, gothic fashions for preadolescents. So I mentally gave you that name. It sort of stuck." I shrugged. "Sorry."

She smiled. "I like it. Raquel isn't my real name anyway. Let's keep it."

I leaned closer, her smile fueling my idea. "Listen, Emily. If you help us solve this murder, then I promise to try to help you." I wanted to tell her she wouldn't have to spend the rest of her life running from a drug-dealing, abusive husband, but I didn't have the resources to give that assurance. I wasn't even sure what I could do, but I could at least try.

"Ah, Polly." Spencer put his hand on my shoulder. "Are you sure?"

Spencer was probably reading my mind as I was his, but neither of us wanted to speak in front of Emily. How could we know for sure that she hadn't done the gruesome deed?

My hero had come to save me from myself. I sent up a silent prayer, hoping that I wasn't getting in too deep with this woman.

I put my hand over his. "Yes."

"But what more can I do to help you? I've told you everything I know."

Spencer cleared his throat. "You said you took back what was yours. May we see the ring, please?"

Emily brushed her hair out of her face. "Sure, I never put it in the safe-deposit box after finding it on Alec. I was too scared that it would link me to him if anyone knew about it." She unzipped her luggage.

I thought of Hillary. I still didn't know who'd hit her over the head. It could have been Emily, and if Emily found out that Hillary had seen the ring, Hillary could be in more danger.

As Emily rummaged through black clothing, I was surprised to spot some bright articles mixed in.

"Here." She yanked out a cloth bag and dumped the contents on the bed. Among various expensive-looking jewels, we spotted a ring that left no doubt as to its tremendous value.

Seeing it triggered an alarm inside. Why hadn't I considered this before? "Is it possible that your husband could have found out about your online chats? And since you've left him, what might he think? Certainly he'd be furious, jealous. But if you took the jewels, he might want them back. They're worth a fortune."

"So, you're saying that if he didn't come after me because he wanted me, he'd come for the jewels?"

"I didn't mean to put it like that. The jewels add another danger to your dilemma."

CHAPTER ⛩ EIGHTEEN

Sure, the jewels provided for Emily if she needed money and knew where to sell them, but she had put her life in more danger by bringing them.

She appeared to grapple with an appalling thought. "Do you think he could have killed Alec?"

The picture she painted of her husband made for a scarier villain than I'd faced so far. Goose bumps crawled down my legs and over my arms. "I don't know how he could have known that Alec had the ring, so it doesn't seem very likely."

The clock on the side table read twelve fifteen, reminding me I'd told Mom to expect me within the hour. I was late. But I wasn't finished with Emily yet. "In the meantime, why don't you stay with me in my room?"

She gave me a questioning look. "But why—"

"You'd be safer staying with us." I had to convince her to stay, at least until we solved the mystery. "Mom won't mind. It might be a bit crowded at first, but we'll figure something out."

"I'm not so sure about this. It would just be putting off the inevitable. Eventually, my husband will find me."

Spencer blocked the door. "Though that might be true, you could have more on your heels than your husband—you could have the authorities. What we know about you now could be enough—"

"I gotcha. You don't have to spell it out." Emily furrowed her brows and rubbed her arms, pacing. "What are you going to tell your mother?"

"I'll think of something." I wasn't happy with how things were working out, but I had to keep both sparrows in the same cage. I needed to go get Mom, but I wasn't sure I trusted Emily alone with Spencer. She seemed bent on appealing to his chivalrous side with her pouting, needy eyes. "Spencer, why don't you keep a lookout in the hallway while I—"

"While you what, Polly? I'm not letting you go anywhere alone."

"That's awfully brave of you, my prince, but who's going to protect Emily?" *Or keep her from running away?*

"Tell me, what exactly are you going to do?"

I brushed past him and put my hand on the knob. "I need to get Mom. That'll give us enough time to think about how to proceed."

"Miss Perkins. Polly?" Emily sounded exhausted. Maybe her disguise had finally taken its toll.

"Yes?"

She stood staring at me, wringing her hands again. "I want to apologize to you. I feel terrible about this, but. . ."

Her words put me on edge. I knew I wasn't going to like the rest of what she had to say. "Go on."

"I was in your room, searching to see if you'd taken photographs of me. I saw you at the Terrace Café yesterday. It looked like you were taking pictures of me again. I planned to delete them if I found them. But then the housekeeper came in."

"You? You hit her over the head?"

She nodded.

Her confession made me fear that she'd done the same to Alec, that she'd lied to us.

"But why did you hurt Hillary?"

"I know what this must look like, but you have to understand how desperate I was. My only intention was to delete any photographs you'd taken that included me."

I thought to repeat my question about Hillary, but keeping silent sometimes elicited more answers.

"I was afraid of what she might think if she found me in your room. I only meant to knock her unconscious."

"Well, you did that. But why did you put her in the closet?"

"I was scared. I wasn't thinking." She sent doleful eyes toward Spencer.

Did that tactic really work these days? She seemed to try too hard to convince us. Or rather, Spencer. Her actions made me wonder about her story of running from her husband.

"On the contrary, you *were* thinking." Bravo. Spencer hadn't fallen for her wounded-soul technique either. "You figured since someone had done that already, then they could get the blame for the housekeeper, too."

My turn to fill in the blanks. "Then you came back last night to destroy my camera and computer."

"No, I didn't come back. I was too scared. That's when I decided to check out of this place first thing this morning, because it was no longer safe. I'd already answered questions from the rangers. They had no reason to keep me."

"But they have every reason to keep you now. You're in up to your neck. Still, you claim you didn't kill Alec." If she was telling the truth, then my initial suspicion that Mom destroyed my computer and camera were back in place. But that would mean she had to have broken into my room in her sleep. It didn't make any sense.

The room seemed stuffy all of a sudden, so I pulled the curtains apart and opened a window. "First, Hillary hits Alec on the head and leaves. If you were telling the truth about what you found, then you would have come into the room after Hillary left. You found Alec in the closet and took the ring."

Spencer picked up where I'd left off. "So when Hillary returns, she also finds him in the closet. Polly, you're just getting to your room. That's when Hillary screams, and you also go next door."

The phone rang. It was Mom. "Look, can I move up to your room now or what? You talked me into getting out of my room today, but now you won't let me leave. So I'm coming up there whether you like it or not. Then we're going to explore this park."

I cringed, frustrated because we were in the middle of putting together the puzzle pieces of the murder. But I knew Mom's insistent tone, and she wouldn't take anything other than a yes from me. I'd learned from the best, after all. Remembering her luggage, I realized it might be better if Spencer went to get her instead of me. "Okay, but I'm sending Spencer to get you. Stay there." I hung up, turning to see Spencer's flat smile. "You heard?"

"Yes. We've got to think fast. What are we missing? Who are

we missing? How could someone have come into the room in between all the other comings and goings? They would have had to have killed Alec after Hillary left and before Emily entered. Think, ladies."

That afternoon, I'd taken more photographs at the lake and then looked around a bit for Mom. I must have been too preoccupied to pay attention to anyone other than her. "Emily, do you remember seeing anyone in the hallway?"

She shook her head. "No, I was too nervous, thinking about having to confront the man who'd stolen my ring. What if I was wrong, and he didn't do it? What if he lied? I just sort of melted behind a plant in the lobby, wishing I'd worn green instead of black."

I almost laughed, but three hard sneezes kept me from it.

"See, all that late-night cavorting, and now you have a cold." Spencer grabbed a glass from the dresser and went into the bathroom.

"It's not a cold. I'm allergic to something. I think it might be your perfume."

Emily's eyes widened, making me feel terrible that I'd insulted her. Then she bolted from the bed. "I've got it!"

Spencer came out of the bathroom, the glass now filled with water. "What?"

"There was a distinct odor in Alec's room that made me think of the holidays. It was an odd smell."

Disappointment registered on Spencer's face. He went to my desk to fiddle with my broken computer.

Something niggled in my mind. "She might have something

here. Was it like turkey and dressing? Spices? Apple and cinnamon? Pumpkin Pie?"

"I wouldn't know, really. Just reminded me of the holidays. I'm not much of a cook. But it's not something I smell very often. So that's why I noticed it while I was looking around the room for my ring."

"I smelled that before, too, here at the park. I just can't remember where." Perhaps I hadn't noticed it in Alec's room because I'd almost immediately seen him in the closet, and that had consumed my thoughts. But Emily had time, while searching the room, for her mind to absorb her surroundings before she'd finally discovered Alec.

The room seemed to grow smaller by the minute. "I wish we could get out of this place." I glanced at Emily. "But I suppose it's too dangerous if you're dressed like yourself. Listen, Spencer, you'd better go get Mom before she tries to lug all her stuff over here on her own."

Spencer stretched, obviously feeling the need to escape, too. "Quite right. But I don't want you going anywhere while I'm gone."

"I promise I won't. Emily and I are going to piece things together."

When he walked through the door, I had the strange urge to kiss him—a simple peck on the cheek—wishing him a good-bye. Not so strange for a wife or a girlfriend, but I feared we weren't at that place yet.

I mentally ran through everything I'd done since arriving, every place I'd been and every person I'd talked to. Someone knocked on the door. I threw my hands up. "See? That's probably Mom now. Spencer couldn't have gotten there and back."

I opened the door before looking out the peephole. "Rene?"

My friend and bride-to-be stood in the doorway, her hair looking freshly shampooed and her face glowing. "Polly. You ready to go?"

"Um, ready to go where?" I moved back to allow her in.

With a frown, she strolled past me into the room. "Conrad and I agreed that we should give ourselves time apart this afternoon, to build up anticipation for tomorrow. So I scheduled us to get our nails done—you know, acrylics. I've hiked almost every trail, so that's out of the question."

Nature girl? "Are you out of your mind? You don't get your nails done. As a matter of fact, neither do I." I scrutinized my pathetic cuticles.

"I know, but I thought on this one occasion, I'd try to become a little more of what Conrad might like me to be."

Shaking my head, I strode toward her. "Conrad doesn't want you to be anyone other than who you are."

She tossed her purse on the bed, realization dawning on her face. "Oh! I didn't know you had company."

"I'd like you to meet my friend Emily." And it was true. Emily was becoming a friend of sorts. "Emily, this is Rene. She's getting married tomorrow afternoon."

Emily's luggage was open, clothes strewn on the bed. She quickly sat on the cloth bag to hide the jewels.

Rene's gaze stopped on the display. "So, is she staying with you or something?"

"Um. . .yeah, it's just for one night." *So far.* How did one keep the truth to protect others without telling lies?

Rene turned her back to me for an instant. I shrugged in apology at Emily.

"Oh." Rene pushed her bottom lip into a pout and plopped on the bed opposite Emily. "And here I thought we could spend some time together. You being my maid of honor."

"Me? Your maid of honor? What about your sister?"

"Oh, Polly, really. Where have you been?"

"Where have *I* been?" A long, deep breath helped to hide the incredulity in my voice. "Where have you and Conrad been?"

"We did some hikes. I told you. Plus, we had to meet with the preacher who's performing the ceremony. Premarital counseling."

"Well, I've stayed close to the lodge." My head was spinning at her sudden appearance. I was in no mood to wrestle with guilt, but there it was. I'd come here for her wedding. With all that had happened, I'd almost forgotten my reason for being in Caldera National Park. And if she needed me to spend time with her. . .

How was I to manage Rene and still follow up on the clues? For that matter, how could I photograph the wedding and be maid of honor? "But what about your sister?"

"She fell and broke her leg. I just found out this morning. I was freaking out at first, thinking it was another omen, but Ronni convinced me that I shouldn't postpone. Conrad agreed, of course. And then I remembered our little talk, and I'm really going to put all that superstitious stuff behind me this time. For real."

Astounded, I stared at Rene. Had she really come that far? "I'm so proud of you." I couldn't help myself; I pulled her into a hug. But remembering what brought on her news, I released her.

"Oh, I'm so sorry about your sister!"

"I know. Isn't it crazy? But don't worry, Polly. She'll be fine."

Honestly, I couldn't believe Rene appeared so calm, but I had no intention of fanning the flames of panic.

"Uh, Polly. But her not being here means, tag—you're it."

I shook my head. "But how can I be your maid of honor?"

"Look, Polly, it was tough deciding between you or my sister to begin with. But it's a small wedding and. . .well, she's my sister. What I'm trying to say is, it would mean so much to me for you to do this."

Rene's words touched my heart. Forget that she didn't have many choices at the moment. "Yes, of course I'll do this for you. But I'm the photographer, remember? And what will I do for a dress?"

"As for the photography, you're talented. I'm sure you'll figure it out. As for the dress, I have that with me. Now are we going or what?" Rene examined her nails, dismissing my earlier objections.

I sighed—my head spinning with my newest responsibility—and looked at my plain, unenameled, short nails again. "I still don't get why it has to be nails. Can't we do something else?" I wanted to pull my hair out and scream. Why now? Spencer would be back with Mom any minute.

"Look, it's my wedding day. I want to be every woman, okay?" She stood and looked at Emily as though trying to decide what we'd do with her.

And that was my problem as well. "Give me a minute to get myself together. Where can you get your nails done around here? I don't think they have nail salons in Miller's Point, do they?"

"It's not too far, Polly, don't worry."

Considering we were in the middle of nowhere at this park, courtesy of Rene's desire to have her wedding here, I ventured to ask, "What exactly does 'not too far' mean?"

While posing the question, I considered what to do with Emily and Spencer and Mom. What would Rene think if she saw Mom moving into my room, too? I'd have to explain everything to her. But the way things were shaping up, that might be the best thing to do.

"Medford, Polly. We're going to Medford." Rene gave a nervous laugh. "All things being relative, that isn't too far. It's about an hour's drive, but I thought we could use the time to catch up."

"I see." That would never do.

"Polly, you can't get your nails done." Emily spoke up, a surprise to be sure.

Both Rene and I stared at her, but if I'd been more than an amateur at this game, I would have acted like I knew why I couldn't get my nails done, going along with Emily.

"You've got that fungus, remember?" Emily pulled my hands out and looked at my nails.

"Oh, ew! You're right. I totally forgot. I can't believe I forgot this terrible fungus I have. It's on my toes, too. Do you want to see?" The truth was, I did have a problem with nail fungus once. Still, I wasn't being completely up front with Rene, and all these half-truths were beginning to eat at my stomach. I chewed the inside of my lip and prayed for guidance.

Rene backed away.

Emily gave a slight shake of her head. What? Was I overacting?

I sneezed again then grabbed a tissue. Suggesting I had a cold would have been a better idea.

Rene opened her mouth. "But I'm not talking—"

"Thanks for reminding me, Emily. We'll have to do something else, Rene. Unless you really have to get your nails done."

I wondered if Conrad would want to spend time with Spencer now, too. We'd come here for them, but the wedding threw a fifty-pound bag of rice—or was it birdseed now?—into my sleuthing plans. Still, maybe there was a way I could make things work. Some of the truth might go a long way.

"What's going on, Polly? You're acting strange." Rene pursed her lips.

What had I been thinking, trying to fool Rene? She'd always been sharp. But desperate times called for desperate measures, or so they say.

I lowered my voice. "It's Mom." Both Rene and Emily came closer. I sighed deeply. "She's been sleepwalking. I'm worried about her, so I'm moving her in with me." I glanced at Emily and continued. "And Emily for tonight."

Rene frowned. "That would be much too crowded for me."

"I have an idea. I don't feel comfortable leaving Emily and Mom to themselves, so would it bother you, Rene, if they tagged along with us?"

Behind Rene's back, Emily shook her head and frowned.

"Well, I suppose we could still spend time together that way. Wait, I know. I still haven't taken the boat ride across the lake. How about we all do that?"

The boat tour. My quick intake of breath drew a sharp glance from Emily. "Sure, that sounds like a perfect idea," I said, my mind wrapping around what could be a way out of this afternoon's plans.

I knew Mom couldn't make the steep trail, especially after taking up smoking again. That would give me a reason to back out, or at least leave Rene and Emily on the boat. I hated scheming like this, but I felt it was for the best and for their protection. The less Rene and Mom knew, the better. And Emily would be safe on the boat tour. Maybe Spencer could go as well.

"That settles it then. I'll go get tickets, and you can wait here for your mom and Spencer."

"All right, we'll meet you in the lobby."

"Depending on what time the tour begins, we can get lunch, unless you've already eaten," Rene said, as she opened the door. "It's almost two. Let's meet at two thirty."

She needn't know the smile I gave her was one of relief. "See you in a few."

The door safely shut behind me, I rested against it. "That was close."

"You're really taking this investigation seriously, aren't you?"

"I feel like I'm this close." I held my forefinger and thumb millimeters apart. "What were we talking about before Rene showed up?" Another painful sneeze erupted.

"I don't remember. Listen, I don't know if you can tolerate me in your room or not."

"That's all right. Rene has allergy pills in her purse. I'll get some when we meet up with her."

I lowered myself to the edge of the bed and blew into a tissue. "I remember what we were talking about. And now I know where I smelled that before."

"You do? Where?"

A knock on the door kept me from telling Emily. I needed to think it through first, anyway. I opened the door for Spencer, who was loaded down with Mom's luggage. I could tell she'd been smoking again. Emily's expression showed displeasure. I wondered if she would try to flee, after all.

I started with explanations before Mom could put me on the defensive. "This is my friend Emily."

Dressed in all white, including a wide scarf that encompassed half her head, Mom smiled, in an attempt to cover her distaste for the all-black gothic look. "Nice to meet you, Emily."

My two new roommates were diametrically opposed. But weren't opposites supposed to attract? Well, I could hope they would at least get along.

Mom watched Spencer set her luggage down, then she noticed Emily's luggage. "Polly! Don't tell me we're all staying here together. I can't do that. Spencer, move me back to my room."

"Mom, it won't be a problem."

She grabbed her toiletry bag and dumped it on the bed. Picking up a prescription bottle, she handed it over to me. "Here. You can have these. I won't take another one, I promise, if you'll just let me go back to my own room."

I was beyond incredulous that Mom had kept another bottle of sleeping pills despite my demands she hand them all over. How many could the woman have? But I refused to discuss that in front of Emily. Feeling Mom was being rude, I gave Emily an apologetic gaze.

"Oh no, no, no. It's not you, dear. It's just that I was already going to suffocate sleeping in the same room with my own daughter. I can't bear to have yet another person in such a small room."

My mind was about to blow. I had so much going on that I couldn't remember why I'd moved Mom to my room in the first place. I shook my head.

Spencer stepped into the fray. "Polly, it's no problem, really." A bead of sweat slid down his temple.

Yeah, right. Between Mom's themes and Emily's black disguises, the amount of luggage Spencer had moved within the last hour should qualify him for some sort of power-lifting competition. I wasn't about to let him move another suitcase.

"We're meeting Rene in the lobby. So there's no time to move again. She's getting us tickets for the boat tour. You and Mom go on down."

Spencer gave me a questioning look before his face became unreadable. "We'll see you there."

After he'd left with Mom, Emily touched my arm. "Look, I'm not sure I should be here. I realize you're trying to help me, but I'm just in the way. I don't have anything to do with Alec. I didn't murder him. I'm hiding from my husband." She wrung her hands. "To tell you the truth, I'm starting to get a little nervous about all this. I think I could hide better by myself. You can't really help me against the likes of him."

"I don't think you have to worry that he's here, because you would have seen him already, right?" What could I say to convince her to stay? I couldn't physically keep her.

"I don't know. I just don't feel comfortable staying in one place for so long."

"Let's talk with Spencer and see what he thinks. Or maybe you

should go to the rangers with your story; they could protect you."
Ranger Jennings's guilt notwithstanding. It was the worst thing I
could have said. Spencer had mentioned going to the authorities
to her, but when I said it, she reacted like I was threatening her.

"I can't do that." She began stuffing clothes back into her
suitcase. "I'm out of here."

"No, wait! I'm only thinking of your safety, Emily. Please!"

She threw her bags over her shoulders and headed for the
door.

I rushed to stop her. "I won't go to the authorities—that's
your call."

"Thanks, but no thanks." Tears brimmed in her eyes. "I know
you wanted to help, but it's not going to work."

Emily opened the door and walked out.

CHAPTER NINETEEN

I'd figured out that the holiday smell Emily referred to was pumpkin pie. I remembered that cloves were among Mom's ingredients for the dessert. I'd smelled cloves on Peter during the boat tour—an uncommon odor to be sure. I once had a friend in college who smoked clove cigarettes. He'd given it up because of a strange lung fungus that occurs in clove smokers. Oddly, my friend had feared contracting the fungus but wasn't worried he could get cancer from smoking. Maybe Peter had never heard of the fungus one could get from smoking cloves. Who knew?

The only other explanation I could think of was he'd been busy making pumpkin pie that morning or had punched an orange full of cloves because he enjoyed the scent. There were many possibilities, but I'd only smelled cloves on one person.

And Emily had smelled the same in Alec Gordon's room.

I dragged myself to the small table at the Terrace Café where Rene, Spencer, and Mom were sitting. Minus Emily. They'd not been in the lobby, but I'd spotted them easily enough. When he saw me, Spencer opened his mouth, but Mom was the first to speak.

"Where's your friend? The girl in black?"

Spencer stood and pulled a chair out for me.

"She had to leave." Blaming myself for Emily's departure made it hard to fully appreciate his etiquette.

Spencer's eyes grew wide. I shrugged again, certain it wouldn't be the last time.

"But I thought she was staying overnight?" Rene asked.

"She changed her plans." I'd almost said she'd received an emergency phone call from home. That would have been a blatant lie. I began to worry that if I continued down this road, I'd become a pathological liar. I thought I was doing the right thing by sleuthing. But how did I continue without hiding things, telling lies? I was in dire need of alone time with God.

A waiter set a glass of iced lemonade before me. I'd been thinking strong, black coffee, but I didn't want to hurt Spencer's feelings. He was the only one who would have ordered lemonade for me.

I mouthed a "thank you" at him and took a sip, so he would know I appreciated it. "When is the boat tour?"

Rene perked up, pulling her gaze from a piece of paper she was writing on. "At three thirty. So we have an hour."

I almost spewed my lemonade. "An hour? Then we'd better get going."

Mom protested. "What? Why? It can't be that far, can it?"

I'd only formed a few details of my plan and hoped that was enough. "The tour starts from the other side of the lake. It'll take a few minutes to get there."

No time to eat, we paid for our drinks and headed to my car. I would have to remember to carry protein bars if I were to keep up this schedule. Spencer managed to nudge me as we all climbed in. "What's going on, Polly? Where did Emily go?"

"We can't talk now, but I need you to do me a favor. You and Rene are going to end up going on the boat tour. Without me. I'm going to bring Mom back. I'll explain later."

His look was severe. I forestalled any lectures by getting into the car and starting it. Rene and Mom chatted along the drive, pointing out various aspects of the scenery. At one point Mom shouted for me to watch the road, because looking out her window, she could see right down the rim to the lake. Spencer said nothing, and I had too much to think about to be an active participant in their conversation.

I pulled into the parking lot for the boat tours. It surprised me that Rene hadn't realized that a person had to be in top condition to hike down the steep drop to the boat dock. But on second thought, she'd been a little self-absorbed lately.

"See, we got here in fifteen minutes." Mom eagerly strolled to the entrance. "The tour doesn't start for another forty-five. Polly, you were worried for nothing."

I approached the sign next to the entrance and read in silence. "Um. . .Mom, I think you need to reconsider this. I'm not sure you're going to want to hike this particular trail to the boat dock and then back up."

"What?" She read the sign as well.

Rene pulled her sunglasses back over her hair and read it, too. "Oh, I'm so sorry. I didn't remember this hike from years ago at all."

"Well, hon." Mom shook her head. "You wouldn't even think about it, of course. You're in such great shape."

"We can do something else then." Rene started walking to the car.

"No, wait." I said the words with too much force. "You and Spencer go, Rene. Don't waste the tickets. I'll try to get Mom a refund." I cleared my throat and gazed at Spencer.

He frowned in return. "I'd love to tour the lake, Rene. Let's do it. After all, we're already here." His words came out like he was reading from a script and had no talent.

"Well, all right. If you're sure?" She took Spencer's outstretched arm. "Polly, I'm sorry about this."

"This is your weekend, Rene. I want you to enjoy it to the fullest." And I did, never mind that her complete focus on herself and the upcoming nuptials gave me much-needed time to search for clues.

For the second time, I thought about Conrad and what he must be doing since he'd apparently not contacted Spencer. As they headed for the trail that led down to the lakeshore, Spencer glanced back at me, concern in his eyes.

I mouthed that I would be all right. It seemed that silent mouthing of words was our only mode of communication lately. But what else could we do with all the secrecy and no privacy?

On the drive back, I pondered what to do with Mom now that Rene was occupied.

"So what are we going to do now? I'm relieved you didn't make me hike down to the lake, but mostly because I'm hungry. I didn't have breakfast because you made me pack my bags and wait all morning for you." Mom rolled down the window. The fresh scent of pine filled the car. "Then I didn't have lunch because we had to rush to this boat tour that I'm not even taking."

I glanced her way, feeling like I had not only neglected Rene but also Mom. I hoped she would be able to make it to the coast to see me. I wouldn't be nearly as preoccupied there as I was here, even with a business to run.

"Sure, why don't we grab something to eat? Then we can decide what to do."

"How long do you think the boat tour will take?"

"It takes quite awhile, Mom. I wouldn't expect them back before a couple of hours or more."

"You know, I'd forgotten about that. While the ranger questioned me, you were off on the boat tour. Why didn't you say you'd already been?"

"I didn't want to spoil the fun for Rene. She wanted to go."

"I'm surprised you'd have a friend like that Emily. Where'd you meet her?"

"Mom, the truth is I only just really met her today." I pulled into the lodge parking lot.

Mom's eyes bored into me; I could feel them without even glancing her way. "You have got to be kidding me. You don't even know the girl, and you were going to let her stay with you. With us?"

"Well, she was in some trouble, needed help."

"I've never known you to pick up strays like that."

We hauled ourselves out of the car and headed to the Terrace Café. The place had become our favorite, it seemed. It was either that or the more expensive, fancy restaurant inside.

"I wish you wouldn't call her that."

"She looked like a woman out of her element, dressed all in black." Mom waltzed to the table of her choice.

I followed. "Look, do we have to talk about this right now?" But Mom had nailed Emily. She didn't fit with the way she dressed—something I had sensed the first time I saw her.

If I couldn't help her, I hoped she would find a place where she felt safe. I wasn't one who believed that people should get divorced, but I had no idea what I would do in the same situation, married to an abusive, controlling drug dealer. I looked at the menu, staring at it like I hadn't seen it a hundred times already and knowing that I would only order one thing. I used the time to silently pray for Emily.

Mom flipped the menu closed and slapped it onto the table, probably meaning to let the waiter know she was ready. Déjà vu came to mind, not for the first time this weekend. In fact, this was the exact same table where Mom and I had met on Thursday when she'd announced she wanted to kill "that man." The whole thing seemed surreal, including my hunt for clues.

I'd never eaten so much Hawaiian chicken in one weekend, so when the waiter arrived, I asked for a hamburger. That was safe. Mom seemed intent on staring at the lake. I pushed aside concerns that she could have murdered Alec in her sleep.

Once our food arrived, Mom dug in. If she was that hungry, then I had at least until she finished her burger and fries to think about Peter in Alec's room somewhere between Hillary's fleeing Alec and Emily discovering him in the closet. On the tour, Peter had commented that a better way to kill Alec would have been to push him over the rim. I almost choked on a french fry. I chugged water, trying to wash down the fry and calm my hacking throat.

"You okay?" Mom came around to slap my back repeatedly.

"Mom, I'm not. . .choking."

When I finally eased my cough, she sat down. People were staring. *Please, Lord, let this not be a repeat of Thursday.* I leaned in to whisper, "Mom, even if I were choking, that's not the Heimlich you were doing. That's not how it's done."

"Well, when you were a little girl, that's what I did when you were choking. Worked every time."

Except I was probably not choking, just like I hadn't been a moment ago. But I didn't want to argue. I shoved another fry into my mouth, trying not to get distracted from my last thought. When Peter commented on a better way to kill Alec, had he been referring to himself in retrospect? I couldn't shake the idea. I coughed again and glared when Mom looked like she might get up to slap me.

Peter had taken me to the lookout—a name that escaped me at the moment—just so he could ask what I'd learned. Then he'd pointed me to Ranger Jennings. Could it be that he'd wanted to frame Ranger Jennings for a crime he'd committed himself? But who would have had greater motivation to kill the man having an affair with his wife than her husband, the park ranger? If Peter had killed Alec, then what was his motivation?

Considering Peter's reaction—a decidedly emotional one—when he talked about his brother-in-law having an affair, I decided that if Peter was involved in the murder, it had everything to do with Hillary's affair. But how and why?

"Mom, after we finish lunch, would you mind if I make a visit to Hillary Jennings?"

"Who's that?"

Too late, I realized I'd never told Mom about discovering the woman in my closet. She'd been sick the whole day or sleepwalking. "Um. . .one of the housekeepers at the lodge had an accident. She's the woman who found Alec in the room next to mine. I want to visit her, and as far as I know, she's still in the infirmary. Do you want to come with me?" I held my breath and wondered how many times people had asked that question just to be polite.

"You go on without me. I've had enough time out of my room as it is."

I almost laughed. "Mom, you're not a dog that needs to go back in her crate for a certain amount of time."

We finished our meal without any sort of performance to speak of, which amazed me. I walked with her back to the room we now shared. Once inside, I closed the door behind me. "If you have any more of those sleeping pills, I want them now."

She stared at me and blinked before turning her face away. I detected a slight rolling of the eyes, which made me feel once again like I was the mom and she the teenager. "Mother, need I remind you what happened last night? Hand them over."

"Oh, all right. But I'm so tired, and I don't think I can sleep without them."

"Well, watch television or something. It's the middle of the day. You don't have to sleep." I thrust my hand out, waiting for the pills. "I'll check on you as soon as I get back from seeing Hillary."

She handed over two more prescription bottles. I widened my eyes in horror. "Mom! What on earth are you doing with so many? These can't be legal, can they? What doctor would prescribe so many at a time?"

"You have them. Now go." She stomped into the bathroom and slammed the door.

"Okay, fine. But this isn't over. I had better not come back and find you zonked out, you hear me?" I gave Mom a hard time because I loved her dearly. And she knew it. I left our room and walked the grounds while I gathered my thoughts.

I reviewed the information I had. Granted, most of it was taken on the word of others. There was nothing concrete in what I knew. But I decided the only person who needed to lie was the murderer, and at some point, the lies would become evident. I cringed at the thought, wondering how many I'd told to cover my sleuthing.

Hillary stated she'd hit Alec over the head. Emily said she found him dead in the closet, and Hillary said the same after she'd come back in a few minutes. What if Peter had gone into the room and found Alec on the floor unconscious?

Peter's words resounded in my thoughts. *He was a scoundrel. Deserved to die. Any man who'd cheat on his wife or with someone who's married deserves no better.*

That had to be it. Peter came into the room and found a person he thought was a scoundrel lying on the floor unconscious, so he finished the job, because to Peter, Alec deserved to die. But how would Peter know that Alec deserved to die?

Hillary might have the answer to that.

I had no idea if Hillary would still be at the infirmary, but I started there. I didn't think she'd be at work yet, and I wasn't sure where she lived. Nor did I want to run into her ranger husband. I needed to figure things out before then. For all I knew, he'd been looking for me to ask more questions. He'd promised to only yesterday. And since he hadn't yet, what could that mean?

I strolled into the infirmary. When I found the room where I'd visited Hillary before, the door was cracked. I knocked lightly and entered. She was getting dressed and motioned me to close the door then turned her back to finish buttoning her shirt. "I told them I wouldn't go all the way into town to the hospital. So they let me stay here for monitoring. Joyce stayed with me through the night to keep me company."

"Joyce?"

"She's one of the medical assistants and a friend. Knew I didn't want to go home or be alone here." Fear laced her voice.

"Why wouldn't you want to go home?" Wouldn't she want to be home with her husband? She'd be safe there. Or would she? "Hillary, who are you afraid of?"

She whirled on me, looking ready to fillet me alive. "Well, who do you think? The killer, of course. He thought he'd killed me. But I'm still alive." A sob broke her lips. "Cliff didn't come back to see me last night or this morning. He's gone. Something to do with the investigation."

So that explained why I hadn't run into the chief ranger. "Well, you can rest easy. I know who hit you over the head. It wasn't the killer. Just someone who is scared like you."

"What are you talking about?" Confusion filled her face. "Then why don't you report whatever you know to my. . ."

She didn't finish her sentence, obviously remembering that I knew more than she wanted to share with her husband. "I haven't seen your husband to tell him anything. But I think he knows about your affair."

Covering her mouth with both hands, she slumped onto the bed. "How do you know that?"

"I suspect, that's all. Who else do you think knew about your affair with Alec?"

Hillary stood and made up the small bed then fidgeted with

the blanket before sitting again. "There was one other person who knew. My husband's best friend."

A new person had entered the equation. I shook my head. "His best friend?"

"He runs the boat tours on the lake."

Peter. With that, I knew my suspicions had been correct. Everything fit. To think I'd gone hiking with him, and he'd tried to point me to Ranger Jennings, his best friend of all people.

"Hillary, I need you to be completely honest with me. If I can figure this out, then you won't have to be scared anymore. And I won't have to worry that someone I love will be arrested for a murder she didn't commit."

Wary eyes met mine. "Well?"

"Why did Peter think Alec deserved to die?"

Her ragged intake of breath told me I was on the right path. The blanket seemed to fascinate her as she drew an invisible design. "You don't think Peter could do such a thing, do you? No, I won't believe it."

"Yes, I think he might be the killer. Just tell me what you know. What did he have against Alec?"

"I think he's in love with me. But he's Cliff's best friend, so he would never do anything about it. I know he knew about my affair with Alec, because he confronted me about it. But I don't believe he would kill Alec because of it." She shook her head as though the mere action could change the truth.

What would she think if she knew I'd suspected her husband at one point? It was hard to understand the mind behind a murder, but clues were pointing at Peter, and he even had a motive. "Look, can I help you get somewhere? Will you be going home from here?"

She frowned deeply. "Cliff was supposed to get me forty-five minutes ago. I'll wait for him here. I don't want him to come get me and not be here."

I could wait with her and, when Ranger Jennings arrived, tell him what I'd learned about Peter—though honestly, I didn't want to be the person to confront him with Hillary's affair and Peter's love for her and the subsequent act of murder. Part of me doubted my reasoning, but a quick check to see if Peter had performed his duties as the tour guide during the time when Alec was murdered would go a long way.

I slapped both hands to my face. Spencer and Rene needed a ride back to the lodge, and it was already approaching the time when I should get them. "Well, I'll leave you to wait for your husband. Please try to tell him everything. He needs to know."

Hillary nodded in response, but I could tell by her expression her thoughts were far away. I ran back to my car and sped around the lake to the boat tour entrance, hoping I wasn't too late to pick them up, making them hitchhike back or wait for me. I imagined they would think of all sorts of ways to make me pay.

A face appeared in my rearview mirror from the backseat.

I screamed, slamming on the brakes.

The car slid to the side of the road toward the two–thousand–foot drop.

CHAPTER TWENTY

The car skidded to a stop, the back right tire near the edge. My heart in my throat, I yelled, "Emily!"

Through the rearview mirror, I watched her. Eyes closed, she rested her head against the seat and released a long breath. When she opened them, they brimmed with accusation. "What sort of driving do you call that? You almost got us killed."

I twisted to face her. "Well, you scared me half to death."

Emily slid to the right side of the car and peered out the window. Just in case we were in danger, I probably needed to see how close we were myself before I pulled back onto the road.

"I'm sorry about that, but it was unavoidable. Polly, he's here. My husband is here!" The fear in her words was palpable. "I didn't know where to go, and I had to hide quick. So I got into your car. It wasn't so bad with the window cracked. What am I going to do?"

Part of me wanted to tell her just to inform him she wasn't coming home. But I didn't live in Emily's world and had no understanding of a person like her husband. Thoughts of news programs about wives murdered by their husbands, even after restraining orders, came to mind.

"Well, neither of us can do much if we don't get back onto the road. What do you see out that side of the window? I mean, my back tires are on the road, aren't they?"

She nodded. "I think so."

"Not good enough. I'd better take a look." I started to get out of the car. For safety's sake, I thought she should, too. "You coming?"

She eyed her surroundings, like she was afraid she'd see her husband jump from the trees across the road. "Yeah, all right."

We climbed out of the car on the safe side. I marched around the vehicle. It had always amazed me how they carved roads into mountains. But why did they have to make them so narrow, leaving the road next to a dangerous cliff, especially on the curves?

"I think we're fine as long as we don't slide. Why don't you wait here until I pull back onto the road?"

Her eyes grew wide, bulging even.

"Don't worry. I'm not going to leave you."

The tires spun on the mixture of gravel and sand before they gained traction. Emily climbed into the passenger seat. Once we were on the road again, we both heaved sighs of relief—well, for the reprieve from one calamity. Now, to deal with another.

"I'm not sure what to do about your husband, but I'm headed to pick up Rene and Spencer. I'm pretty sure I can figure out how to occupy Rene with something else so we can deal with your dilemma. First, I'd like to wrap up the murder case."

"Are you that close to solving it?"

"I think so, yes. On the other hand, I'll know soon enough if I have any skills as a sleuth."

I drove into the parking lot where I hoped to wait for Spencer and Rene, not the other way around. Stragglers exited the entrance, breathless in most cases. Spencer came out alone. I jumped from the vehicle and waved, smiling to stifle my laugh when he bent over, grabbing his knees to catch his breath.

I made my way over to him. "Where's Rene? Don't tell me you beat her up the trail."

"No." He stood, still breathing hard. "She and Conrad left me."

"Conrad? What was he doing?"

"He apparently had the same idea we did. Was on the tour. Water?"

"Uh, no. But hey, there's some over there." I dug out some change and jogged to the vending machine.

When I got back, he was already chatting it up with Emily, who'd gotten out of the car. He smiled and walked to the front of the vehicle, taking the bottle from me. After a long swig, he gazed into the woods, a deep frown on his face. He spoke in a low voice. "Where'd you find her?"

"Didn't she tell you? Her husband is here."

After another drink, he said, "Tough luck, that."

I punched his arm. "Spencer. We have to help, of course. We detained her to begin with." I glanced back at her.

Emily had closed her eyes. She reminded me of a frightened puppy.

"Well, I've come to a conclusion." I climbed into the car while Emily moved to the backseat, allowing Spencer to sit up front next to me.

"You mean you know who killed Alec?" He swirled the last of the bottled water.

I looked over my shoulder as I backed out of the parking

spot. "Maybe. But things are growing more dangerous, and with Emily's predicament, I think we need to find Ranger Jennings and tell him everything we know."

I looked in the rearview mirror at Emily as I said the words. Her eyes popped open.

"But what if he's the killer?" Spencer asked.

"I think I know who killed Alec. But it's a sticky situation, and all things being considered, we have to get Emily the protection she needs. Plus, what she knows will help shed light on things."

"Hey, wait a minute. You're talking about me like I'm not even here."

As I managed the snakelike bends in the road, I glanced at her in the mirror again. "I don't see that we have many options here. You need help, and what you told me helped me figure out who killed Alec Gordon. We need to give the ranger this information before it's too late." I punched the gas a little harder, sending us around a corner too fast for comfort.

"Polly, what do you know that you haven't told us? The way you're whizzing around these corners, one would think another murder is about to be committed." Spencer put into words what I couldn't put into a thought.

"Call it a woman's sixth sense, or is it seventh? There was a love square, which is now a love triangle, and I'm hoping to keep it from changing again."

"Huh?" Spencer and Emily voiced their confusion in unison.

I wasn't sure I could explain the entire thing. This whole situation was wearing on me. "Let me put it this way. We need to find Ranger Jennings. I feel like something is about to happen, but I don't know what."

"You don't think they're going to arrest your mum, do you? You didn't discover the strange scent on her, did you?"

"Uh, no." Though I'd put Mom's possible guilt out of my mind repeatedly, Spencer's comment sent a new tendril of fear through me.

I'd been so focused on Peter smelling like cloves that I hadn't even considered Mom with her various perfumes. Because she'd taken up smoking again, the smell masked much of her perfume. Of course, it was supposed to be the other way around. But a thought hit me. Had she taken up smoking cloves and I hadn't noticed, her perfume somehow masking that particular scent? I swallowed, a lump growing in my throat.

Once we arrived at the ranger station, I jumped out of the car and looked in the open window at Spencer.

"Let me go in by myself and see if the ranger is even here. I only see two cars. He could be anywhere. He could be at home with his wife, for all we know. You stay in the car with Emily. She'll be safe."

I trotted up the steps and pushed through the door. A dark-haired ranger with glasses stopped what he was doing at his desk when he saw me and stood. "What can I do for you?"

"I'm looking for Ranger Jennings."

"He's not here. Is there something I can help you with?"

My gaze flicked to his desk. I saw a memory card and wondered if it were mine. "Um. . .probably not. Do you know where I can find him?"

"Sorry, ma'am." He shook his head and focused on the computer screen again.

I asked if he could try to contact Ranger Jennings. While I

told him it was about the murder case, I managed to walk around to see the pictures he was looking at. I recognized them at once and explained that those were my shots.

With that, he took me seriously and radioed. A frown quickly appeared. "Sorry, ma'am, he must be out of range. If you know something, you can tell me."

"I'm not talking to anyone but Ranger Jennings." I marched through the door, got into the car, and sped from the parking lot. I saw him exit the log cabin in my mirror.

"Polly, I don't like this. What's going on? What did you say?" Spencer gripped the armrest and door handle.

"I told him I knew something about the murder, but he couldn't get Ranger Jennings on the radio."

"Why didn't you just tell him everything and leave it at that?"

"Because if I have to explain everything from the beginning in detail, it might take too long. I think something's wrong. We need to hurry."

Once back at the lodge, I said, "Hillary was leaving the infirmary today. I don't know where she lives, but let's go down to the basement and talk to someone there."

We bounded down the stairs to the basement, where I'd first cornered Hillary. The large woman who'd interrupted us in the restroom saw me from inside the laundry room and came out to greet me—a kind way of putting it.

"I need to find Hillary. Can you tell me where she lives?"

"You have the nerve to come here and ask me that?" She put her hands on her large hips.

"It has to do with the murder. It could be a matter of life or death." I could tell by her frown that I wasn't making points.

"If you won't tell me how to contact her, let her know that I need to speak with her. She's a grown woman, she can decide for herself."

I wanted to stick out my tongue, but I resisted, turned, and left. Spencer and Emily followed me. Footsteps above let us know that someone was on their way down the steps. I hoped it wasn't the ranger from the station and almost suggested we turn around when Hillary appeared.

"Oh, thank goodness I found you! Polly, you've got to help me. I told Cliff everything." A sob escaped. "Only it all came out in a jumble. I'm afraid he misunderstood. He's. . .I'm scared."

"Okay, Hillary. Tell me exactly what you mean. Why are you scared?"

"He said he was going to finish things once and for all." She spoke in a high-pitched frenzy.

"Wait a minute. What exactly did you tell him? How did he misunderstand?"

"I told him everything I told you. Only, he thinks I was having the affair with Peter!"

I grabbed her to steady her.

The large woman appeared on the steps below and glared at me. She charged up the stairs. "You let go of her this minute, or I'm going to beat you to a pulp."

Hillary gathered her wits enough to protect me. "May, stop it. Polly's here to help."

I took over from there. "In fact, May, you can help, too. Get her a cup of tea, something to calm her. I've got to find her husband."

"No, I want to come with you," Hillary said.

"Everything centers around you. I think you'll only fuel the fire if you're there."

She sagged into May, who nodded, reassuring me that she would take care of Hillary.

"Where do you think he was going?" I asked.

"To find Peter. He was so angry. I've never seen him like that."

I sped up the stairs, Spencer and Emily in tow. Peter could be conducting a boat tour or at the island. "Spencer, why don't you ask Amber if she knows where Peter is?"

He grabbed my elbow and ushered me to the wall. Holding my shoulders, he peered at me, his face close. "Why do you have to carry this so far? Give the information you have to that other ranger. It's no longer your fight."

What he said hit me hard. Why *did* I have to find Ranger Jennings, stop him from confronting Peter? Peter was guilty, after all. But Hillary made it sound like her husband planned to harm Peter. She almost made me consider Ranger Jennings as a suspect in Alec's murder all over again.

I'd started sleuthing to make sure that Mom wasn't found guilty. Then Hillary asked me to help, and I'd agreed. There was also Emily to consider.

But the real reason I had to do this? "Because, Spencer, if something happens that I could prevent, I'll never forgive myself. Especially since I encouraged Hillary to tell her husband everything. How can I stop now? There's something else. I've always wondered if I'd handled things differently, would Brandon be here today? If I'd not given up on him when, after days of searching, the authorities had? I have to see this through to the end."

His face had been inches from mine, but at the mention of

Brandon, he pulled away. I hoped I hadn't hurt him.

Emily and I waited next to a wall behind a large indoor tree while Spencer found Amber. Emily's eyes were wide as she scanned the tourists, looking for her husband. I hadn't had much time to ask her more about him and felt bad.

"So what does he look like?" Speaking the words made me more aware that I hoped I didn't see him. I wished I were wearing a wig and tattoo at that moment, though he wouldn't be looking for me. I slid behind the greenery a little farther.

"You need to act natural. You look like you're hiding. Come out a little. And put an attitude on your face like this." She allowed her face to go slack and her eyes to roll just enough to look like she was bored out of her mind and hated everyone.

I laughed. "You're very good, you know."

"My husband is tall and good-looking, not unlike your Spencer."

A spark of jealousy coursed through me at her reference to Spencer. I shrugged it off.

"He usually wears expensive suits. But when I saw him today, he was dressed like some sort of mountain climber. I don't know. Wait, like the Brawny paper towel man, that's it."

"He looks like a lumberjack?"

"Today he did. He could have been here for days, Polly, and I wouldn't have known."

Spencer returned. "You ladies look like you're hiding."

"You found us easily enough," I said.

"I suppose that doesn't bode well for you if I could find you. But I have good news. Amber thinks Peter's at the island. She said he likes to take a few of the kids over there after hours to—how did she put it? Party."

"But if Ranger Jennings found him first, he didn't make it. Still, that's our best bet."

"Ah, but you've forgotten something."

I angled my head.

"We need a boat to get there."

CHAPTER ⫿⫿ TWENTY-ONE

"**G**eorge!"

Spencer cocked his head to one side.

"The groundskeeper, remember? He's got a boat. Come on, we've got to hurry." I pushed through the doors, hoping George would be somewhere on the grounds.

"Why don't we spread out? We can find him faster that way." Spencer had made his decision and was already walking in the opposite direction. "I'll meet you back here in twenty minutes."

"Wait, maybe Emily should go with you." I didn't like to think what would happen if her husband showed up. I couldn't possibly protect her against him. Hopefully her disguise would work.

Emily went with Spencer, which I think he agreed to a little too quickly for my comfort.

My twenty minutes of searching the grounds was unfruitful. Doubts assaulted me. I hoped that Spencer and Emily had better luck than I'd had as I made my way back to our meeting place. Spencer was pacing. Alone.

"Where's Emily? Oh no! Her husband didn't find her, did he?"

"No. She saw him first. When we found George, we explained

the situation. He didn't need much convincing. Emily is with him. They've gone to the boat; they're waiting for us."

"Good. Her husband isn't likely to look for her there." Everything was happening so fast. My mind was slowly wrapping around the fact that I was hiding a woman from her husband—albeit an abusive drug dealer. I needed to do the right thing, but I hadn't had enough time to consider what that was. Still, I managed to push that to the back of my thoughts. A bomb needed diffusing, and I'd told Hillary I would help. Strange how things had shifted from protecting loved ones to protecting complete strangers.

Spencer and I made the dreadful hike down the trail to meet Emily and George, who'd gotten a head start on us and had already powered up the boat.

After we climbed in, Spencer looked at me, concern in his eyes. "Polly, have you considered what we'll do if and when we find them?"

The question had niggled at me since we began our search. "All we can do is try to keep another tragedy—another murder—from happening."

Spencer stared at the island fast approaching. "And how can we do that, if, say, either one of them chooses to use a gun?"

I shook my head. "They won't. I believe Peter killed Alec, but I don't believe he's a murderer."

"What do you mean?"

"I think it was a crime of passion, nothing premeditated."

"Still, if this is the other part of a love triangle, there could be another crime of passion. We should have given this to the authorities." He shoved both hands through his hair. "I mean, *other* authorities."

"That's why we're going. To talk some sense into them. There wasn't time to bring in another ranger. We'd have to explain everything, you know."

It was already past seven. Darkness would close in on us before we made it back, I was certain. What was I thinking by doing this? I moved closer to George, cold wind gusting through my hair. I shivered, uncertain if it was from the physical cold or dread. "Do you have flashlights?"

"Dig around in there." He nodded toward a small cabinet door.

I opened the door and shuffled through odds and ends. Spencer joined the hunt. We came up with two flashlights, but only one of them worked.

With an ominous expression, Spencer nodded as the boat slowed to dock. There were two boats already there. I stood up and looked at George, my hand on Emily's shoulder. "Why don't you and Emily stay here? If we don't come back soon, you can go get help."

"We'll wait for you, but if I get a whiff of anything run amok, I'll come looking for you." With that, George pulled a shovel from under his feet.

I wasn't sure how much it would help, but I hoped things wouldn't come to that.

Spencer hopped out of the boat and held his hand out to help me. "You ready?"

"I think so." The gravity of my decision to find Ranger Jennings and Peter finally hit me. My legs trembled. "Which way should we go?"

"Considering he brings the college-age volunteers here, which seems a strange thing to me, we might try looking for them first."

Spencer rushed up the boarded walkway to the path.

He'd pointed out the obvious. He stopped, and I almost bumped into him.

He turned to face me, grabbing my arms. "Listen, Polly. It's not too late to go back. You don't have to do this."

"At this point, Spencer, if we turn back and something happens. . ." I shook my head as images flooded my mind. "I could never forgive myself."

"But something could happen to you, Polly." He peered into my eyes, emotion flooding his gaze. "I'm a fool to have allowed you to investigate to begin with."

Afraid he would convince me, I pushed past him, freeing myself from his arms. "But you couldn't have stopped me."

"No. That's why I asked to be included. You need to let me do the talking tonight, all right?"

Despite the weighted cloud of fear beginning to oppress me, a small grin slid onto my lips. Spencer, my knight in shining armor. He wanted to protect me. I hoped he wouldn't have to.

Fire flickered through the trees, accompanied by the smell of smoke and the sound of jovial voices. Was I asking too much to find both men there? We broke through the trees. Seven or eight twenty-somethings, mostly guys, stood around the fire. A couple of girls huddled on a fallen tree. All of them, sipping from cups. The scene brought back memories. Considering the clutter usually left behind after such get-togethers, I questioned whether this was a sanctioned event. But maybe the summer volunteers were allowed this one deviation. And maybe that's why Peter brought them—to oversee the activity and make sure things didn't get out of hand.

Two guys who stood apart from the group and near the woods where we entered the circle noticed our approach.

Spencer whispered, "I don't see Ranger Jennings or Peter."

The taller of the volunteers frowned, whereas the shorter one smiled and marched over to meet us. "Did you guys get left behind on the island or something? What are you doing here?" He took a drink from his cup.

I caught a whiff—unmistakably beer. "Um. . .we're looking for Ranger Jennings and Peter."

Spencer gave me a sharp look, presumably to remind me he wanted to be in control. I didn't recall agreeing.

The guy's smile flattened. "Haven't seen them."

I could feel Spencer tense. "Now see here, are you saying that the man who brings you to this island isn't here?"

"That's not what I said. I just haven't seen him since we got here. Do you need to get back? Because you're welcome to hang out with us until it's time to go."

Spencer had already started back through the woods. I followed. The sun would be setting soon, and I feared we'd have to use the flashlight after all. "Where should we go now? I don't want to get lost on this island and be left here all night."

"Fortunately it's not that big. The way I see it, we have two choices. We can walk the shore, or we can take a trail."

Wait a minute. I stopped in my tracks, trying to capture the thought hovering just out of my reach. "If I were Peter, I'd probably go to a high point somewhere." Peter had taken me to the lookout the day before; I figured he had a preference for nice views. There was also his comment about a murder looking like an accident should someone fall.

"There's only one of those on this island. If I'm remembering correctly, the cliff is on the other side though. Come on." He glanced back to make sure I would follow.

"Why are we running?" I knew we needed to hurry, but I wasn't sure I could run the steep trail he was leading me on.

"Save your breath, Polly."

He was right. Eventually we both found ourselves out of breath and unable to do much more than hike up the strenuous trail. A steep climb would mean we should find the cliff soon enough. I decided that my idea to take up running at home would not be enough to keep me in shape. But then again, I would probably not venture back to this national park. Ever again.

Spencer put his finger over his lips. We crept out into the clearing—a viewpoint overlooking the lake. There at the edge, just as I'd suspected, stood two men. My heart rate soared, pulsing in my throat. I couldn't know for certain that Peter had murdered Alec, yet here I was about to make that accusation. They hadn't seen us yet. They were caught up in their conversation, which appeared calmer than I'd expected, given Hillary's urgent fear her husband was going to inflict bodily harm on Peter. However, I was more concerned that Peter would decide an accident was in order.

Spencer made to step forward. I pulled him back and shook my head then whispered, "No, I need to be the one to do this."

I'd seen the body, and I'd known Alec. Before he could reply, I jogged forward. Both men jerked their heads toward me.

"You don't have to do this." The words spilled out before I knew it. Both men appeared confused to see me. At that moment, getting them away from the cliff's edge was all I could think about.

"Stay out of this, you meddling—" Ranger Jennings scrunched his lips as though he was biting back a host of uncomplimentary words.

Peter stumbled forward. I held my breath, hoping he wouldn't stumble the wrong way.

Ranger Jennings steadied him as he addressed me. "What are you doing? How did you get here?"

"Hillary was worried and wanted me to find you."

"Why would she send you?"

"Because I know what Peter did, and she was afraid for you."

Peter stumbled again, and I realized he'd had too much to drink. He grabbed Ranger Jennings. "I'm sorry I fell in love with your wife. I've tried to fight it."

Ranger Jennings's jaw tensed, but he kept his focus on me. "This is a private matter. Now, if you'll please go back the way you came. I know everything there is to know."

The two men were acting strangely. I suspected that Ranger Jennings wasn't pointing the murder finger at his friend. "You know that Peter killed Alec Gordon?"

"I didn't do it, Cliff, I swear it." Peter plopped to the ground. "I learned months ago that you and Hillary were having trouble. One night you'd had too much to drink, and you told me you were considering leaving her. That's when I figured I could wait things out. I'd be there for her when she needed me. But then she'd turned to that scoundrel, Alec."

"Enough of this." Ranger Jennings tugged him to his feet.

Peter stared at his friend, if you could call him that. "I even told you about her affair with Alec, thinking you'd leave her sooner and eventually she'd see the light and dump that good-for-nothing. . . " Peter sagged. "But you ignored it."

I'd been so caught up watching Peter, that I hadn't noticed Ranger Jennings standing back, left hand palming his gun. This was exactly what I'd wanted to avoid, the reason I'd come. But there wasn't anything I could do to stop it.

Ranger Jennings said nothing. He waited, as though expecting Peter to say more. Or perhaps he was waiting for him to confess to the murder? "What makes you think he killed Alec Gordon?" He directed his words to me.

I'd hoped that by simply confronting Peter, he would confess. I didn't have too much to go on, so I tried another approach. "Peter, you went into the room, found him on the floor, and thought you'd finish him off, right?"

"No! That's not what happened."

Ranger Jennings stiffened. "Go on."

"The afternoon of the murder, I took my break and came back to the lodge. I was in the hall when I saw Hillary run from a room in hysterics. I knew who she was running from, and I wanted to kill the man for hurting her. All I could think about was punching his lights out. I ran into the room and found him lying on the floor, unconscious." A sob broke from his lips.

Spencer gripped my shoulder and squeezed. I held my breath, waiting for the confession that was sure to follow. A motorboat whirred in the distance.

"With one blow, I could get rid of two people who were hurting Hillary. I thought you'd be arrested—no one had a greater reason to kill Alec than the man whose wife was cheating on him. I'm sorry. I should never have considered it. You're my friend. Please forgive me."

Even in the waning light, I could see the grievous expression on Ranger Jennings's face as he shook his head. "I still love my wife, whatever trouble we may have. I'd never leave her, no matter what. And now, though it hurts me to do this, I have to arrest you for the murder of Alec Gordon."

"What? Wait! I didn't do it. I couldn't go through with it."

Stunned that he'd try to deny it at this juncture, I stepped in again. "Look, we know you were in the room. You confessed you were there, and even if you didn't confess, the scent of cloves was there. Something I smelled on you before. You smoke clove cigarettes."

Peter sobered. "I do no such thing."

Doubt began gnawing at me. What if Emily had killed Alec and lied to us?

I looked out over the water and made out George's boat heading away. "Spencer, George is leaving."

Emily burst from the woods, breathless. She held up a shovel. "It was George. He killed Alec."

CHAPTER ## TWENTY-TWO

Ranger Jennings appeared to tighten his grip on Peter. "How do you know?"

"He was putting clove oil on a cut on his hand. Like an idiot I blurted out about smelling cloves at the crime scene. George stopped what he was doing and stared at me. All of a sudden, I knew it was him. He was the one who killed Alec Gordon." A sob escaped. "And I could see by the look on his face that George knew I knew. I grabbed the shovel for protection and jumped out of the boat."

Emily paused to catch her breath and shuddered. "I barely got away, but as soon as I was on the dock, he took off." She gazed at the shovel, as though only now realizing she'd carried it all the way up the hill. But who could blame her? The girl was scared to death.

Stunned, I looked at Peter, feeling guilty and embarrassed that I'd accused him.

He scowled at me, hurt in his eyes. "His wife had given me clove oil for a nasty burn. That's what you smelled on me that day."

"Let's go." Ranger Jennings led the way.

All five of us trekked down the hill. It was growing dark fast. Although Ranger Jennings and Peter still had much to resolve, for now, a murderer had to be caught. Peter stayed with us while Ranger Jennings arranged for someone else to give the rim volunteers a ride back.

The boat took off, churning through the water. By now we operated fully on headlights, but Peter and the ranger knew the lake well enough. Once at the dock, they had to leave us, because I wasn't able to keep up. Spencer assured them he would see us to safety. They left to run after George.

I thought I knew who'd committed the murder, but I'd missed the smallest of clues. I'd thought of George as a friend of sorts. He'd even driven us to the island.

Why had he killed Alec Gordon? The questions raged, and I still had to hike up the trail. Once we were back at the lodge, we found Rene, Conrad, and Mom waiting for us in the lobby. They'd witnessed George's arrest. After many warm hugs and much explaining, we bade each other good night. Mom and Emily went with me to my room.

Somehow, now that the murder was resolved, I felt the experience was anticlimactic. I'm not sure what I'd expected from my first attempt at sleuthing, but it had been a complete disappointment, except, of course, for the fact that Mom was no longer a suspect.

But lest my heart grow hard, I reminded myself that Alec Gordon had been murdered this weekend. I'd spoken to him beforehand, which had brought up the bitterness I'd held toward him. Maybe God had given me that opportunity to set my heart right. In lieu of that, I realized now, I'd also wanted to solve his murder as a way to redeem myself from my own crime—a crime of the heart.

Only Jesus could redeem me, could set me free. Finally I allowed Him to do just that. I forgave Alec, though already gone, and asked God to forgive me. While I was on the path of recovery, I also forgave Spencer for hurting me all those years ago. I put the ghosts from my past to rest.

The next morning was Sunday—W-day. Rene would be wed to Conrad in a few hours. After breakfast we headed to the parking lot. Still reeling from my failure to pin the murder on the right person, I was surprised when Ranger Jennings approached while we piled into cars to attend the nearest church service.

He stuck out his hand. "I wanted to thank you."

A bit startled, I took it. "For what?"

"George Hamilton wasn't even a suspect. Without your nosing around, I'm not sure we would have caught Alec Gordon's killer. At least as soon as we did."

The heat of embarrassment flooded my face. "I was glad to do it."

Hillary's whack with the lamp hadn't killed Alec. Instead, George's shovel—the very same one he'd had on the boat—had done the gruesome deed. Apparently George wasn't one to stand by and watch people hurt others. He'd already been searching for Alec with a quarrel stuffed in his pocket just like his rag, when he found him on the floor. He'd been planting trees in the atrium inside the lodge that day and carried the shovel with him. For some inexplicable reason, he'd moved Alec into the closet after banging him on the head with the shovel. Maybe he'd planned to retrieve the body later and bury it somewhere in the vast park.

Early on, I'd compared Mom and myself to pawns in a game. I was thankful she'd not participated in this one. With so many people coming in and out of the same room, I'd pictured that door opening and closing as if revolving. But though they'd all seen the body, they hadn't seen each other. It reminded me of the movie *Clue*, the comedy based on the board game.

I still didn't want to believe that George had committed murder. But George had lost many jobs due to his temper, a side of him I hadn't seen except in the one photograph—the one George had tried to destroy on my computer and camera.

After church, we made the mad dash back to the lodge, where Emily and I assisted Rene with her dress. Rene had joined in my cause to help Emily. She seemed less anxious now, if only a little. We gladly included her in the wedding ceremony. Emily would stand in for Ronni. Rene thought it would make quite a story to tell their children. I was more than glad, because I hadn't had time to locate the sort of tripod I'd need to both photograph the wedding and stand up as her maid of honor. A more-than-dashing Spencer in his tuxedo gave me trouble concentrating as it was.

Wedding vows were said and before I knew it, Spencer, Mom, Emily, and I were in the parking lot, bidding Rene and Conrad farewell. They planned to hike the Pacific Trail. Certainly not something I'd want for a honeymoon, and I suspected even with Spencer's many travels, it wasn't his cup of tea either.

Though the wedding was a small, formal event, Ranger Jennings and Hillary had been invited to attend. After watching the lovebirds get married, Hillary shared that she and Cliff planned to get marriage counseling.

Though the long weekend had started on a bad foot, even Mom had good news: Her lawyer assured her she would get her money back. And if I were reading Mom's sudden happy mood correctly, there might be romance in the air where her lawyer was concerned.

With plans to head back to the coast after the wedding celebration, I still needed to check out of my room. Mom and Emily had already gone back inside the lodge. Spencer stood next to me and sighed. I hated for my time with him to end. What did this mean for us?

Three state police cruisers, sirens whining, screeched into the parking lot. Spencer grabbed me, pulling me out of the way, next to a tree. Several officers, Ranger Jennings included, shuffled a handcuffed man from the lodge. He looked like the Brawny paper towel man. Emily followed close behind. They stuffed the man into the back of a vehicle as she sobbed into an officer's shoulder.

Spencer and I shared a bewildered look.

"Maybe the drug dealing caught up with him." Spencer took my hand and pulled me close.

"I suppose, but what is Emily going to do?"

"At this minute, I only care about what you're going to do." He pressed his lips against mine.

Elation infused me all the way to my toes, making me feel like I was floating. The kiss ended too soon.

"Well, are you going to visit me at Bradford Court, my parents' estate?"

"That depends on if you're asking me to come see you, or

you're just offering me another old house to photograph."

He held me even tighter. "I'll take whatever I can get."

As my head rested against his shoulder, I sighed. I could stay there forever. "The Goonies 'R' Good Enough," theme song to the movie *The Goonies*, resounded from my jacket. I'd long forgotten my cell phone in the pocket.

"It's working now? How weird is that?" The number was a New York prefix. I hated ending the quiet moment with Spencer, but I took the call.

Spencer's eyes brightened when I hung up. "You look happy. Who was that?"

"A magazine editor. I e-mailed some photos of the lodge along with an article idea."

"Sounds like you might have a new career."

"Uh-huh. And sounds like Bradford Court might be just what the editor ordered."

Spencer winked. "Jolly good."

Elizabeth Goddard is a seventh-generation Texan who recently spent five years in beautiful southern Oregon, which serves as a setting for some of her novels. She is now back in East Texas, living near her family. When she's not writing, she's busy homeschooling her four children. Beth is the author of several novels and novellas. She's actively involved in several writing organizations including American Christian Fiction Writers (ACFW). She loves to mentor new writers.

A Letter To Our Readers

Dear Reader:
In order that we might better contribute to your reading enjoyment, we would appreciate your taking a few minutes to respond to the following questions. We welcome your comments and read each form and letter we receive. When completed, please return to the following:

Fiction Editor
Hometown Mysteries
PO Box 719
Uhrichsville, Ohio 44683

1. Did you enjoy reading *The Camera Never Lies* by Elizabeth Goddard?
   ❏ Very much! I would like to see more books by this author!
   ❏ Moderately. I would have enjoyed it more if _____
   _____
   _____

2. Where did you purchase this book? _____
   _____

3. How would you rate, on a scale from 1 (poor) to 5 (superior), the cover design? _____

4. On a scale from 1 (poor) to 10 (superior), please rate the following elements.

   ____ Heroine   ____ Plot
   ____ Hero   ____ Inspirational theme
   ____ Setting   ____ Secondary characters

5. These characters were special because? _____

_____

_____

6. How has this book inspired your life? _____

_____

_____

7. What settings would you like to see covered in future
Hometown Mysteries books? _____

_____

_____

8. What are some inspirational themes you would like to see
treated in future books? _____

_____

_____

9. Would you be interested in reading other **Hometown
Mysteries** titles? ❏ Yes   ❏ No

10. Please check your age range:
    ❏ Under 18   ❏ 18-24
    ❏ 25-34   ❏ 35-45
    ❏ 46-55   ❏ Over 55

Name _____

Occupation _____

Address _____

City, State, Zip_____

E-mail _____

Other
HOMETOWN MYSTERIES
from Barbour Publishing

Nursing a Grudge

Missing Mabel

Advent of a Mystery

Nipped in the Bud
October 2010

May Cooler Heads Prevail
November 2010